"This is your wake-up call," Dan Blair chuckled as Beth answered the phone in Room 113 of the Sunrise Inn in Great Falls.

"I've been up since five o'clock," Beth replied. "I was too excited to sleep. Just think, in five hours I'll have Jeffey in my arms again."

The drive to Sweetgrass from Great Falls was uneventful, and the hours seemed to drag by. Beth felt like a little child every time she asked, "How soon are we going to get there?"

They arrived at the Customs' Office in Sweetgrass at eleven forty-five. Beth paced nervously across the lobby, inspecting every car approaching the check station. No one who was traveling with a small child fit the attorney's general description.

"Would you like a cup of coffee while you wait?" the customs agent asked as he sensed her nervousness.

"Yes, that would be nice," she replied as she waited while he filled a styrofoam cup for her. As she was taking her first sip, a brown Bronco stopped in the parking lot. A young man in a business suit got out along with a well-dressed middle-aged woman. The woman opened the door to the back seat and unlatched a child's car seat. She took the child by the hand and walked around the back of the vehicle toward the lobby of the inspection station.

"Jeffey!" Beth shouted as she ran out the door and across the parking lot just as fast as she could.

The child broke away from his caregiver's hand. "Mommy!" he shouted as he ran toward her with his short legs moving just as fast as they could.

ANN BELL, a librarian by profession, lives in Billings, Montana, with her attorney husband. Ann has worked as a teacher and librarian in schools in Iowa, Oregon, Guam, as well as Montana. Previously she has written numerous articles for Christian magazines and a book titled *Proving Yourself: A Study of James.*

Books by Ann Bell

HEARTSONG PRESENTS
HP66—Autumn Love
HP89—Contagious Love

Inspired
Love

Ann Bell

Rocky Bluff Chronicles: Book Three.

Heartsong Presents

This book is dedicated to the memory of two great Montana women, Monida Vaughn and Muriel David. Their "kitchen table" ministries served as a model for the character Edith Dutton.

A note from the Author:
I love to hear from my readers! You may write to me at the following address:

> Ann Bell
> Author Relations
> P.O. Box 719
> Uhrichsville, OH 44683

ISBN 1-55748-668-9

INSPIRED LOVE

one

The co-manager of Sleepy Eye Motel in Rocky Bluff, Montana, forced a smile as the young, slender stranger approached the desk. "May I help you?"

The weary traveler glanced nervously around the lobby. "I'd like to rent a room with a kitchenette," he snarled.

Anita Reed shuddered. "We only have three kitchenette units and they're generally full, but someone just checked out this morning so Number Thirteen is available." She reached for the room key behind her and the registration form under the counter.

The young man reached for a pen and began filling out the form. A scowl crossed his face. "I hope it's on the back side of the building. I don't like being disturbed."

"Yes, it's right off the alley. It'll provide you with a lot of privacy. How long do you plan to stay?"

He nervously took a round can from his hip pocket. He opened the container and placed a small wad of tobacco in the side of his mouth. "I'll be in Rocky Bluff until I decide to move on."

"Our policy is that the kitchenette units must be rented for a minimum of three days," Anita stated firmly. "After that it can go on a day-by-day basis with the check-out time at eleven o'clock."

The stranger took his wallet from his tattered GI fatigues and handed her a hundred dollar bill. "Take the first three days out of this."

Anita counted back the change and then reached for the partially completed registration form. She glanced suspiciously over its contents. "I'm sorry, sir, but you didn't fill out your model of car and license plate number."

He grabbed the paper back and reached for the pen on the counter. "Boy, you hick-town people sure are snoopy. It's none of your business what kind of car I drive."

"It's one of our regulations. It also helps us provide better protection for our guests." Anita breathed a sigh of relief as her husband entered the side door of the lobby.

The disgruntled traveler scribbled a response on the form and handed it back to Anita without muttering another word.

Anita handed him the key to room thirteen. "Have a good day. If there's anything we can do to make your stay more pleasant, please let us know." Her kind words did not betray her inner fear and concern.

Grabbing the key, the young man stomped from the room, oblivious of Dick Reed's presence.

Dick shook his head with disgust. "Boy, he's a mean acting dude to be driving such a late model Porsche. Most Californians leave their fancy cars behind and only bring their all-season vehicles when they come to Montana on vacation. Generally, they want to see the beauty of the back woods, not try to impress the natives."

Anita glanced out the window. "I wonder what he's up to here in Rocky Bluff," she responded. "We're too far off the normal tourist route between Yellowstone and Glacier Parks for casual visits."

"I think we'd better keep an eye on him. If he does anything suspicious we ought to let Phil Mooney know down at the police station. I heard that Little Big Horn County is seeing a great increase in drug traffic. There's a lot of flat land here for traffickers to land small, private planes."

Anita looked quizzical for a moment. "I have heard a lot more low-flying planes lately, but I just assumed they were crop dusting."

"That's what they want us to think, except it's long past the spraying season. I just hope that our new guest isn't one of them. But drug money could explain the fancy car."

&

Beth Slater arranged a pile of toys on the kitchen floor and then joined Edith Dutton at the table for a leisurely cup of coffee. "I hope Jeffey won't be in your way if he plays with his trucks in the corner."

"That's perfect," Edith assured the young mother. "It's been such a pleasure to watch Jeffey grow. It doesn't seem like any time at all since you brought him over for the first time. He was all wrapped in blankets and spent most of his time sleeping in the corner."

A faraway gaze settled on Beth's face. "I don't think I could have gotten through those early days without you. I often wonder what would have happened if you hadn't been working the crisis line the first time I called it."

"I'm sure the good Lord would have brought someone else into your life at that time." Edith paused as memories of the last four years flooded her. "I'm just glad I was the one who got to know you and little Jeffey. It's been so encouraging to watch a scared sixteen-year-old learn to care for her baby, then get her high school diploma and go on to take secretarial courses at the community college."

"At the time I never thought it would be possible, but here I am getting ready to go on a job search myself." Beth took a long, pensive sip of coffee before continuing.

"When Libby Reynolds graduated and got her first job as a paralegal it all looked so easy. Now when it's my turn to go out into the workaday world it seems so difficult. I don't even know how to begin."

Edith handed Jeffey another chocolate chip cookie. Before she retired as the home economics teacher of Rocky Bluff High School, her recipe for chocolate chip cookies had become famous throughout the state of Montana. Her cookie jar was rarely empty.

Jeffey dropped his matchbox truck and reached for the cookie. "Thank you, Mrs. Dutton."

"You're welcome, sweetie," she replied. Edith turned her attention back to the proud mother. "I'm glad to see that you're teaching manners early to Jeffey. It makes it so much easier when they get in school."

Beth's baby was growing into a normal, happy child. "Jeffey seems to have been born with a sweet spirit," Beth beamed. "I'm so glad you directed me to the necessary social services when I needed them. But now it's time I get off welfare altogether," she declared. "Edith do you have any tips on how to begin job-hunting?"

"Have you tried to put a resume together yet?"

"How can I prepare a decent resume when I've never had any job experience? And no one is going to give me a job without experience."

"You've taken care of Libby Reynolds's baby regularly," Edith reminded her. "That would count toward demonstrating dependability and responsibility."

"Hmm. I never thought of that."

"If you listed the skills you've learned in your various classes you'd have a lengthy list. Why don't you sit down tonight after Jeffey's asleep and jot down the highlights of each class?" Edith suggested. "We can go over it in a few days and compile a list of your qualifications and draft your resume so all you'll have to do is go to the computer center and type it."

Beth glowed as a weight of concern was lifted from her shoulders. "I sure appreciate your help," she replied. "Will you be busy Wednesday afternoon to go over the details?"

"I'll be here," Edith assured her. "How does two o'clock sound?"

Edith went on to remind Beth to read the job ads in the *Rocky Bluff Herald* newspaper every day and to stop at the Montana State Job Service at least once a week.

Beth nodded her head in agreement with each suggestion Edith made. "And, most importantly," the older woman continued, "do as much volunteer work as you possibly can. You never know what might turn into a full-time position."

"Libby's volunteer work on Stuart Leonard's election committee for County Attorney sure won her a jewel of a position," Beth giggled. "I don't know where to begin looking for a volunteer position. I faint at the sight of blood so I wouldn't be any good at the hospital."

"I volunteered at the crisis center when I first retired," Edith reminded her with a twinkle in her eye. "In fact, I found more than just a few hours of fulfillment. That's how I met Roy. We were married several months later."

Beth sighed as her shoulders slumped. "I wish something like that would happen to me but I don't think there's much of a demand in Rocky Bluff for single mothers as wives."

"Don't give up hope so soon, you never know what the future will hold," Edith consoled as she patted Beth's hand.

"Just go on with your plans and Mr. Right will sneak into your life in the most unexpected way."

Beth straightened her shoulders as Edith's wisdom reached deep into her spirit. "You're right," she smiled. "The most important thing right now is finding a job so I can support myself and Jeffey, and get off welfare."

Beth paused and took another sip of coffee before continuing. "Several months ago the director of the crisis center asked me if I would have time to help with the clerical work there. I was too busy with classes then, but from now until I find a full-time job I could probably help at least once a week."

"That's perfect," Edith replied enthusiastically. "Why don't you give Dan Blair a call when you get home? We could then include your volunteer work on your resume."

Just then Jeffey crashed two trucks with disgust. Beth motioned for him to stop and then began helping him pick up his toys and placing them in his bag. "Edith, you've been a great help, but I think I better get Jeffey home for his afternoon nap. It looks like his frustration level is getting too high."

Edith fetched Beth's and Jeffey's coats from the front closet then helped the four-year-old get his arms into the sleeves. "I'm looking forward to our visit Wednesday," she said as she opened the door for her guests.

Beth smiled. "Thanks. I need all the help I can get. I'll take your advice and give Dan Blair a call as soon as Jeffey is down for his nap."

Edith watched the young mother and child from her living room window until they rounded the corner. *So many troubled young people have found their way to my kitchen table for encouragement since I retired,* she mused. *My heart attack may have slowed my body, but as long as my welcome mat is out I don't have to feel trapped within these walls.*

Returning to the sofa, Edith reached for a pillow, slipped off her shoes, and stretched out for a quick nap. As soon as she had dozed off she was awakened by the shrill ring of her telephone. *I wonder who that could be?* she thought as she rubbed her eyes and hurried to the phone.

"Hello, mother," Jean Thompson greeted when Edith picked up the receiver. "How are you and Roy doing today?"

"I'm doing well, just my usual slow self," she responded with a chuckle. "However, we're having trouble getting Roy's diabetes stabilized. One minute he's fine, the next minute his blood sugar may drop to a dangerous level. Last night it zoomed up to four hundred again."

"Has he been staying on his diet?" Jean queried. "I know how much Roy likes his sweets."

"Surprisingly enough he's followed his diet religiously, so I don't understand the fluctuation," Edith stated. "It sure is nice having a nurse for a daughter to share my concerns with."

"At least my advice is free," Jean laughed. "However, maybe you should notify your doctor and not wait for his regular appointment."

"I suppose you're right," Edith sighed and then searched for a way to ease the tension building within her. "Now enough about us. How are you and Jim and Little Gloria?"

"We're doing great. I enrolled Gloria in nursery school three days a week while I work and she loves it. She brings home all kinds of artwork for our refrigerator."

Edith grinned. "I hope you'll share some of it with me,"

she said. "When Jay and Dawn were little, Bob and Nancy made sure I was supplied with all kinds of 'Grandma's Art'."

"Mom, do I still have to keep competing with my big brother?" Jean teased. "My kid's artwork is as good as his kids."

"Don't be ridiculous. I'm just saying I like to see the work of all my grandchildren, not just those who live close by," Edith scolded gently and then took a deep breath before continuing. "Not to change the subject, but how's Jim doing? I hope the problems at the sawmill are being resolved."

"I wish they were," Jean replied, not able to hide the pain in her voice. "The environmentalists won," she stated sadly. "The spotted owl controversy was enough to close the area woods from logging, which is forcing all the saw-mills around Chamberlain, Idaho, out of business. It's really a sad time for our town. I don't know if it will ever be able to recover."

"Does Jim know what he's going to do yet?"

"Since he's working in the office he'll be one of the last ones to leave. He has to make sure all the financial accounts are balanced before they lock the doors. Then I don't know where we'll go. There's already talk of having to close the local hospital because of declining support. That means I'll be out of a job as well."

"If you do decide to leave Chamberlain, it sure would be nice if you'd move a little closer to Rocky Bluff. It's aw-fully hard to have family so far away."

"We'll have to see what happens. I'll call you in a few days and let you know what's developing," Jean replied. "Mother, promise me you'll call the doctor about Roy," she added as she ended the conversation and returned her phone to its cradle.

Edith had just made herself comfortable in her recliner when Roy came out of the master bedroom to join her. "You sure have had a busy afternoon," he said, brushing his lips against her cheek. "Who was that on the phone?"

"Jean just called to let us know the mill where Jim works will be closing and they'll probably be looking for jobs somewhere else."

"I sure wish they'd move back here. I'm getting kind of attached to Gloria," Roy commented as his eyes sparkled. "She's getting to be a real charmer."

"That's exactly what I told her." Edith paused as her eyes caught a glimpse through the window of Bob's Ford Taurus pulling into the drive. "I wonder what Bob's doing here in the middle of the day?"

"I guess we'll soon find out," Roy replied as he opened the front door for his stepson. "Bob, glad you could stop by. What brings you out at this time of day?"

"Coffee break time," the dark-haired businessman countered as he made himself comfortable on the sofa. "Besides, I need some words of wisdom from mother and you."

Edith raised her eyebrows as she remembered the days when Bob wanted sole control of the family business that Bob's father started more than thirty-five years before. *Bob has changed so much since the car accident that killed Roy's son, Pete, she thought. That guilt nearly destroyed Bob before he came to terms with his responsibility.*

"Mom," Bob began as he surveyed his aging mother. The wrinkles around her eyes and forehead seemed deeper each time he saw her. "Since the grand reopening of the store after the fire I'm finding myself in an extremely unique situation. With the settlement of the insurance company and the extra business that has been generated I'm going to have to invest in a hurry or pay a tremendous tax bill. Do you have any ideas?"

"For someone who was contemplating bankruptcy just a little over a year ago, this is a major miracle," Edith chuckled. "Just off the top of my head my only suggestion would be to open a satellite store. Your father always wanted to do that but the cash flow was never there at the right time."

Bob scratched his head and stared out the window for several minutes. "That's a good idea," he said thoughtfully. "But where would I build it? Great Falls and Billings are crowded with hardware stores."

"Bob, why don't you try one of the smaller towns around here?" Roy suggested. "All of them cater to the farmers and ranchers, but no one is willing to invest in their towns. The business people want the major cities and the retirees and new transplants all want the mountains. No one seems interested in the foothills and the prairies, so that's a ripe market for investment."

Bob grinned from ear to ear. "That's a fantastic idea. I could do a little investigative work as to the local economy and the support a new store might expect to receive from the locals. Do you have any suggestions for location?"

Edith mentally scanned the geography of central and eastern Montana. Suddenly her eyes brightened. "How about Running Butte? It's only a little over an hour's drive from here. It's a well-kept little town with a lot of community pride, even after they closed the school and bussed the children into Geraldine. The reservation towns are often neglected by the outside world."

"Hmm, not a bad idea," Bob replied as he stroked his chin. "Maybe Nancy and I will drive out there this weekend and look around. Would you and Roy like to come with us?"

Roy and Edith exchanged glances. "Sounds good to me. I'm always looking for a chance to take the prettiest woman in town out to the countryside," Roy chuckled.

"Oh, by the way, Bob," Edith inserted. "Your sister called this afternoon. It seems that the environmentalists temporarily won the battle in the Northwest and shut the woods up for logging. They're going to be closing Jim's mill. The entire town of Chamberlain is pretty upset about their loss. Right now Jim and Jean don't know what they're going to do. However, with Jim's accounting skills I'm sure he'll be able to find another job but I'm sure it will mean they'll have to relocate."

"I wonder how they would like to live in Running Butte," Bob snickered as he slipped on his coat and headed for the front door.

two

"Pretty flashy car for someone hanging around Rocky Bluff," Lieutenant Philip Mooney commented. He and Sergeant Scott Packwood were passing the Pizza Palace on the way back to the police station after investigating a minor traffic accident.

"I've seen that Porsche parked at the Sleepy Eye Motel the last couple of nights when I've had graveyard patrol," Scott replied. He peered through his side window hoping the driver would return to his car. "I hope they're just here on vacation and not someone trying to bring in drugs. We've had a lot of suspicious activity lately that we just can't put our finger on."

"Let's keep an eye open for the driver, but we have to remember just because most young people in Rocky Bluff drive a pickup truck, it's not a crime to drive a Porsche," Phil chuckled.

The pair rode in silence for the next couple of blocks as they surveyed the community which they were proud to protect. "Phil, isn't that Beth Slater coming out of the Job Service Building?"

"Sure is," Phil replied. "I wonder if she's trying to get a job. She sure has been working hard to improve herself. She went to night school to finish her high school education and then took a secretarial course at the college. I don't mind paying taxes to help people like her get back on their feet."

"I know Edith Dutton has taken her under her wing and provided her a solid role model," Phil observed. "It's amazing the impact a few quiet people can have on this community. Edith has proven to the rest of us that age and physical limitations don't keep a person from influencing troubled youth."

Unaware of being watched, Beth turned the corner and headed for the Dutton residence. The crisp fall breeze whipped through her hair as it rustled the leaves around her feet. Jeffey was staying with a friend while she began her first official day of job hunting. The Job Service clerk had told her about a vacancy at the high school. Beth could hardly contain her enthusiasm. Could this be the lead she needed? Only an expert in the field would know, and she could hardly wait to see her.

Roy Dutton had just returned to the living room from finishing lunch when he noticed Beth hurrying up their front walk. "Edith, Beth is here a little early this afternoon. Judging by the way she's walking she's pretty excited about something."

"I hope she has good news about a job," Edith responded as she went to open the door for her young friend. "She's been working hard enough to get one."

Before Beth had a chance to ring the bell, the front door of the Dutton home flew open. "Beth, do come in," Edith invited. "I'm all ready to help you with your resume."

"I'm sorry I'm early," Beth explained as she took off her jacket. "I got a lead at the Job Service and I can hardly wait to talk to you about it."

Edith smiled and motioned for her to follow her to the kitchen. "Let's have a cup of coffee while you tell me about it."

"Getting this job would be an answer to my prayers," Beth confided as she made herself comfortable at the kitchen table.

"So where is it?" Edith teased. "Don't keep me in suspense."

"It's at the high school. They are looking for a clerk-secretary in the library to begin the first of November. The Job Service counselor said the woman who has this position now is moving to Denver."

Edith thought a moment while she poured two cups of coffee. "That would be Jenny Jones's job. I did hear that her husband's trucking firm was doing some reorganization and he was being transferred. She did an excellent job keeping the library organized when I taught at the high school."

"Hmm." A puzzled look spread across Beth's face. "Jenny Jones? Didn't I meet her a long time ago at a cosmetic party you hosted?"

"I forgot about that," Edith admitted. "She was here that night. She's a sister of Patricia Reagan who use to do volunteer work at the Spouse Abuse Center."

"Well, tell me more about the job," Beth urged. "It's sounding better all the time. I especially like the idea of having summers and holidays to spend with Jeffey."

Edith passed a plate of cookies to her guest. "Rebecca Sutherland is the librarian. You'll enjoy working with her," the former home economics teacher stated. "She has about twenty-five years of library experience with twenty of those here in Rocky Bluff. It wouldn't surprise me if she retires before too long."

"Well, do you think I've had the right kind of training for the job? I don't want to apply for a job I couldn't handle."

"With all the computer classes you've had you'll be a 'shoo-in'," Edith encouraged. "I heard that the school just received a grant to automate the library and that means there will probably be a lot of data entry. They say it's a pretty complex procedure to enter the entire card catalog into the computer."

"Then in my resume I better emphasize my computer skills," Beth replied as she took a pad and pen from her oversized purse. "I'll need to come up with some profound objective for desiring this job. I obviously can't say I just want to earn money," she chuckled.

Edith beamed. "It looks like you came prepared."

"I've been giving this a lot of thought," Beth admitted. "In fact, I went to the public library this morning and photocopied some samples of different formats of resumes." She reached into her purse and took out six pieces of paper folded in half. "I think I like the top one the best, but the second one isn't bad."

In an hour both Edith and Beth were satisfied with the rough draft they had tailored specifically for the Rocky Bluff High School library position. "Since Jeffey's at the sitter's I'll have time to run over to the computer lab and type this now. I can file my application at the school the first thing in the morning."

Beth rose and began putting on her coat. "Edith, thanks for all your help. If I get this job it will only be because of your help."

"If you get this job it will be because of your own hard work," Edith reminded her. "If you need a good recommendation be sure and use my name."

❧

Saturday afternoon an oversized moving truck stopped in

front of the home of Bob and Nancy Harkness. Twelve-year-old Dawn rushed out the front door. "Hi, Uncle Jim. I've been waiting all day for you," she exclaimed as she gave Jim Thompson a big hug. "When are Aunt Jean and little Gloria going to get here?"

"They had to stop for gas so they should be along shortly. Is that big, mean dad of yours home?" he chided.

"Dad said to have you call just as soon as you got in and he'll come right home. I think there may be some change of plans," Dawn explained.

Just then Jean and Gloria drove up in the family minivan. Jim and Dawn hurried to the curb. "Hi, Aunt Jean. How's Gloria?"

"We'll find out in a moment," Jean laughed as she gave her niece a squeeze. "She's been sleeping ever since we left Missoula. It's time to wake her or she'll never go to bed tonight."

When Jean opened the car door next to the sleeping child the cold blast of fall air brought her to sudden alertness. "We're here," Jean whispered as she lifted her daughter from her car seat.

Within minutes after Jim called him, Bob joined his sister and brother-in-law in his spacious living room. "I'm glad you were able to pack up and move so quickly," Bob said as he poured a cup of coffee for each of his guests. "I didn't expect this deal to go through so fast."

"That's one of the few benefits of renting and not owning a home," Jim replied with a touch of sarcasm in his voice. "However, we're now going to be home owners. . . sort of."

"I'll have to admit it was kind of nerve wracking to select a double wide mobile home sight unseen complete with floor plan and colors," Jean said. "The colors were rather limited, but I think we'll be happy with what we bought. We did want an extra bedroom in case we have an addition to the family before long."

"Are you trying to tell me something?" Bob teased.

Jean shook her head. "Not yet, but don't be surprised."

"So when's the mobile home coming?" Jim asked as he took another sip of his coffee. "We don't want to impose on you too long."

"The workers brought it in yesterday and they're assembling it today. It sure simplified things to be able to find a lot that already had a septic tank and electricity," Bob explained. "Why don't we take your van to Running Butte tomorrow afternoon and see how it's coming along? If they're done I'll take off work Monday and help you unload your truck."

"Sounds good," Jean replied. "Maybe we could take Mom and Roy along. I'm sure they need an outing."

"They do keep busy, but I sense they feel trapped since neither one is able to drive any more."

"How have they been doing lately?" Jean queried. "When I've talked to them on the phone they've sounded a little discouraged."

Bob shook his head. "Mom's been busy helping anyone in town who seeks her out. However, Roy seems to be slowing down an awful lot."

Jean wrinkled her forehead. "She told me several weeks ago that they were having trouble keeping his blood sugar under control. If we go out of town we'll have to be sure to take his insulin in an insulated kit and have some extra sweets in case he has a problem. I'm sure the fresh air and ride in the country will do him a lot of good."

"I think we'd better let them know that we're in here," Jim chuckled. "It doesn't take long for word to spread that a moving van is in town. They would be awfully hurt if they knew we were here and didn't go to see them."

Bob hurriedly gathered up the coffee cups and placed them in the sink. "Mind if we take your van so we don't have to move the car seat?"

"I was just getting ready to offer."

Just as Jim was turning onto Main Street a shining black Porsche sped around them. "Where did he come from? It sure looks like the locals are getting mighty prosperous in the last few months."

"Sorry, that one has California plates," Bob observed with a note of cynicism. "We're not getting many California escapees in this part of the state, but the Gallatin and Flathead Valleys are having real growth problems. Their infrastructure can't adapt to such rapid change all at once and our state coffers are too broke to help them out. I don't know how it's going to turn out. I'm just glad I live in Rocky Bluff."

"That's an interesting phenomenon," Jean noted. "Montana use to be the place for only the most hardy, and few people paid any attention to us. Now it's become the ideal escape from big city problems."

&.

Both Roy and Edith were dozing in their recliners when their family entered through the back door. "Mom, we're here," Jean shouted.

"Come on in, everyone," Edith replied as she adjusted her chair to the upright position. "We were wondering what time you would be getting in. We'd like to treat everyone to dinner at Beefy's Steak House tonight."

"That will be a treat," Jean replied as she leaned over to kiss her mother. "Are you sure they are prepared for a three-year-old?"

"I've seen more poorly behaved children than her eating there," Edith laughed. "Besides, my grandchildren are always good. Right, Dawn?"

"Right, Grandma," she giggled as she held her cousin's hand tightly.

Roy finally aroused to alertness. "Hello, everyone. Glad to have you back in God's Country for good," he chuckled. "How are the plans coming for the store at Running Butte?"

"We're on a roll," Bob assured him. "One reason why I wanted Jim and Jan here long before the store actually opened was to become familiar with the community. Since Running Butte is next to an Indian Reservation we need to know how best to stock the shelves to meet their needs. The land over there isn't nearly as productive as it is around Rocky Bluff."

"I'm looking forward to working with the Native Americans," Jean added. "I heard a rumor that a new medical clinic is coming to Running Butte and I'd like to get in on the ground floor of that project."

"That sounds exciting," Dawn exclaimed. "Maybe someday I can come up and help you."

"I'd like that," Jean assured her. "Your schooling has to come first, but maybe you could come for the summer and help with Gloria."

಩

Monday morning while Beth was doing the breakfast dishes she was interrupted by the shrill ring of her telephone.

"Hello."

"Hello, may I speak with Beth Slater, please."

"This is she."

"This is Viola Tomkins, the secretary at Rocky Bluff High School. The administration has reviewed your application and the principal has asked me to set up an interview time for you. Would you be available at three o'clock Wednesday to meet with Mr. Walker and the librarian?"

Beth could hardly believe her ears. She had worked and prayed for this moment and now she was nearly speechless. "Yes. . . sure. . . I'll be there Wednesday. Thank you for calling."

Beth hung up the phone and picked up her startled child and danced around the kitchen.

"Mommy, what happened?" Jeffey asked, barely able to talk beneath her bear hug.

"I have an interview for a job," Beth explained as she set him back on the floor. "That means we'll have enough money to buy a car and get some of the things we've never had before."

"Can we get a fancy black car like the one we saw going down the street yesterday?" he begged.

Beth giggled. "We won't be able to afford anything that fancy, but maybe I can find a matchbox car like the one you saw. It was so far away I couldn't see the exact model, but maybe we could match it up pretty close."

Beth picked up the phone and dialed a familiar number. "Hello, Edith," she greeted when she recognized the voice on the other end.

"Well, hi, Beth. How's it going?"

"I just got a call from the high school and they want me to come for an interview on Wednesday. Isn't that exciting?"

"I'm so happy for you," Edith replied as she sat down in the chair next to the phone. "Grady Walker called me as a reference late yesterday and he was extremely impressed with your training at the community college. I take that as a very positive sign."

Suddenly Beth's voice softened. "I won't know what to say. I've never had a job interview before."

"Just be your usual sweet self and answer their questions. Mr. Walker is a friendly kind of person. There's nothing to be afraid of."

"The librarian will also be at the interview," Beth explained.

Edith chuckled. "Don't worry about Rebecca. She's the kind of person who can put the most fidgety neurotic at ease."

"If that's the case, I'll feel right at home immediately."

❧

Wednesday afternoon, dressed in her best Fashions by Rachel dress, Beth dropped Jeffey off at a friend's house and walked the six blocks to the high school. The thought of having a car of her own made the distance seem even longer. Promptly at three o'clock she was ushered into the administration office.

"Hello, Beth," Viola greeted. "Would you like to have a seat? Mr. Walker got detained with a parent, but he'll be free in just a few minutes. Can I get you a cup of coffee while you wait?"

"Thank you. I'd like that," she replied as she made herself comfortable on the padded chair. *So this is where all the excitement happened,* Beth mused. Knowing Larry and Libby Reynolds now it didn't seem possible that he could have shot Mr. Walker. *It's amazing how life has gone on as if nothing happened. I wonder if Mr. Walker still flinches every time he sees an unruly student walk through his door? It takes a mighty big person to forgive someone the way he forgave Larry.*

Beth's thoughts were interrupted by a tall, middle-aged man. "Hello, Beth. I'm Grady Walker. I'm sorry to keep you waiting, but I had a minor crisis occur right before you got here. Won't you come in, please?"

Beth obediently followed him into his office. She surveyed his cluttered office and the family pictures on his desk. He must be extremely proud of his family, she thought.

A well-dressed woman in her late fifties rose as she entered the room. "Beth, I'd like you to meet Rebecca Sutherland, our librarian. Rebecca, this is Beth Slater."

Rebecca extended her right hand. "It's nice to meet you."

The trio sat at a round table in the center of Mr. Walker's office. Beth found herself immediately at ease as she explained her background and experience with clerical work and computers. Finally, after an hour of discussing Beth's qualifications and explaining the job responsibilities, Mr. Walker said, "Beth, I'm sure you're anxious to see the library. We're mighty proud of it since we moved it into the new Edith Harkness wing. Rebecca will give you a grand tour. We'll make our decision this evening and will be in touch with you in the morning. Thank you for your time."

When Beth entered the spacious, well-lit library she immediately understood why they were so proud of it. Everything was clean and organized with the latest audio-visual equipment lining the walls.

"As Mr. Walker told you we're planning on automating next year, so for the next few months we're going to be placing bar codes on all the books," Rebecca said.

"That's going to be a massive job," Beth noted, as she tried to estimate the number of books on the shelf.

"That it will be, but I'm sure we can finish before the school year is over," the librarian assured her.

Beth felt as if she was floating on clouds as she walked to her friend's house to pick up Jeffey. She had only been at Rocky Bluff High School for a little over an hour and yet she felt she was already a part of that institution. *Imagine me, Beth Slater, four years ago a high school dropout, possibly being offered a job in a high school,* she thought as she crossed the street.

Suddenly her thoughts were brought back to her immediate environment as a black Porsche sped past her, nearly bumping her off the curb. "Crazy driver," she mumbled. "Why don't you watch where you're going? Don't you know pedestrians have the right of way?"

ও

The hours passed slowly that night as Beth tossed and turned in her bed. *Did I get the job or didn't I?* she wondered. *I felt like the interview went well and they liked me, but I don't know who else applied for the job. There are thousands of people out there who are a lot more qualified than I am.*

The next morning Beth busied herself baking cookies as she waited for the phone to ring. At nine fifteen the phone rang. Beth hurriedly wiped her hands and reached for the receiver.

"Hello."

"Hello, is this Michael's Computer Store?"

Beth's heart sank. "I'm sorry you have the wrong number."

Beth went back to her cookies. Each minute seemed like

an hour. Exactly at ten o'clock the phone rang again.

"Hello."

"Hello, is this Beth Slater?" a man's voice greeted her.

"Yes, it is."

"This is Grady Walker. I would like to offer you the job of clerk-secretary of the Rocky Bluff High School library. Are you still interested in the position?"

Still interested? Beth could hardly contain her excitement. "I'd be delighted to accept. Thank you for your offer."

"Good," the principal replied. "Could you be at work November first at eight o'clock? Report directly to my secretary. She'll have some paperwork you'll need to fill out. I'm looking forward to you joining our school family."

three

"The workmen on the new store sure started early this morning," Jean Thompson observed as she prepared breakfast in her new double-wide mobile home. "They're a dedicated bunch."

Jim smiled as he peered out the kitchen window. "That's one of the advantages of hiring local help. The unemployment rate is so high on the reservation I have a waiting list for workers. It probably won't be long before other businesses will recognize the eager supply of labor and relocate to Running Butte as well."

· "The plans for the new medical clinic are nearly finished and I imagine they'll be ready to build about the time the store is complete," Jean said as she placed three bowls of oatmeal on the table. "I think they're planning to do about the same thing Bob did... bring in a pre-constructed metal building and then hire local help to complete the interior. The weather is so unpredictable here, the less outdoor work the better."

Jim spread homemade strawberry jam on his toast. "These metal buildings can get pretty hot in the summer, but with air conditioning it shouldn't be a problem."

"Hopefully we'll be open before spring planting begins," Jean replied. "I was in the grocery store yesterday and overheard some locals talking. They're looking forward to not having to drive one hour each way just to buy a handful of nails."

"That's what I like to hear. It's going to take a lot of community support to make this work," Jim paused. "At first I was concerned they might not be as supportive of non-Indians, but I guess I can put that fear to rest."

Jean leaned over and picked up a piece of toast that Gloria had tossed on the floor and then turned her attention back to her husband. "I talked to Bob last night and he's going to bring the entire family up this weekend to inspect the progress. Hopefully, Mom and Roy will be able to come with them. I'm planning on a big dinner for my official house warming."

"Sounds good to me," Jim said as he glanced at the clock. "I better get out there and get to work," he chuckled as he stood and pushed in his chair. "I don't want to be labeled as 'one of those lazy outsiders'."

≈

As soon as Grady Walker called, Beth Slater could scarcely contain her excitement about obtaining her first job. She immediately picked up the phone and dialed a familiar number.

"Hello, Edith," she exclaimed as soon as she recognized the voice on the other end of the line. "I have great news, but I don't want to share it over the phone."

"I can hardly wait to hear it," Edith responded. "Why don't you bring Jeffey and come on over? Can you have lunch with us?"

"Thanks," Beth replied, as she eyed her son playing on the floor. "We'd like that. Jeffey always likes to go to his Granny Edith's house."

Beth hurried into her bedroom to freshen up and then put clean clothes on Jeffey. She packed a toy bag for him, grabbed their coats, and headed for the Dutton residence.

This news was too good to wait.

Edith was watching for them as Beth and Jeffey came up the front steps. She flung the door open before Beth had a chance to ring the doorbell. "Hello, Beth. . .Jeffey. Do come in out of the cold."

"That fall wind is kind of nippy. I hope we don't have a storm moving in," Beth replied as she removed her coat.

"Mommy got a job and we're going to get a car," Jeffey blurted as soon as he walked in the door.

Edith beamed and looked at Beth for confirmation.

Beth nodded. "Grady Walker called this morning and asked me if I wanted the clerk-secretary job in the library."

Edith hugged her young friend. "When do you start?"

"The first of November. I have so much to get done before then."

"I'm sure you'll be able to do all that has to be done," Edith encouraged. "Let's go to the kitchen and make some plans. I guess the obvious question is, who'll take care of Jeffey while you work?"

"I know several women who take children into their homes, but at Jeffey's age I'd rather have him somewhere he'll get preparation for school," Beth explained. "I know I'm biased, but he appears to be extra bright for his age."

"That's not prejudice," Edith chuckled. "That's a statement of fact."

"I've heard some of the mothers in my classes at the community college talk about Kinder University Day Care. I thought I'd go by there tomorrow and talk to the director. It's just three blocks from the high school so I could walk over and see Jeffey on my lunch break."

"Sonya Turner and Patricia Reagan are codirectors of the day-care center. They have a pretty good thing going for them," Edith replied, as she poured them each a cup of coffee. "They used to be volunteers at the Spouse Abuse Center. While they were there, they saw that the biggest need of this community was adequate day care. I've only heard good things about them."

"The only thing that bothers me about going to work is that I was just beginning to do the clerical work at the crisis center for Dan Blair. I'll hate to let him down. He's swamped with paper work."

"Since you'll be off work at three-thirty every day, maybe you could spend a little time after work at the crisis center. Why don't you go down and talk with Dan and see what can be worked out?" Edith suggested. "When I was doing volunteer phone work there, I found everyone extremely accommodating to the various work schedules of the volunteers."

Beth paused for a moment before she spoke. "That's a good idea. Tomorrow after I go to Kinder University I'll stop and see Dan. The crisis center was responsible for me getting my life turned around so I'd really like to give back as much as I possibly can."

❧

The next day Beth Slater lifted the latch to the front gate of Kinder University. The yard was full of brightly-painted play equipment. One teacher was supervising eight children as they scampered around the yard, each bundled in a heavy coat and hood. Jeffey's eyes brightened. "Can I go play with them?"

Beth beamed. Her son seemed to love the day care on first sight. "Maybe later," she replied. "First we need to talk to someone."

The young woman by the swings quickly approached

Beth and Jeffey. "Hi, may I help you?"

"Yes. I'd like to talk to the director about possibly enrolling Jeffey in the center."

"Great. We still have room for several more children," the teacher replied. "Either Patricia or Sonya can help you. If you ring the front door bell, one of them will be right with you."

Beth rang the bell and within moments a young woman dressed in stylish slacks and a sweater came into the doorway. "Hello," she greeted. "May I help you? My name is Sonya Turner."

"Hi, I'm Beth Slater. I think we met several months ago at a cosmetic party at Edith Dutton's," Beth said as she extended her hand. "I just got a new job and I wanted to check into enrolling Jeffey in day care."

"That's right. I remember you now," Sonya smiled. "You were considering taking classes at the community college at the time but were afraid you wouldn't be able to make it. Do come in."

"Well, I did take those classes and it wasn't nearly as bad as I thought it would be," Beth responded, immediately feeling at ease. "In fact, because of them I was able to get my first job."

"Great," Sonya smiled as she led the way to her office. "Maybe Jeffey would like to play with the others while we talk."

That was all the invitation the four-year-old needed before he was right in the middle of the other children. The rocking horse with a rope mane held the greatest appeal.

Sonya and Beth visited as if they were long lost friends. Sonya explained their procedures and day-to-day routine and Beth shared some of Jeffey's interests and favorite foods. Within minutes Beth was certain this was the right environment for her son. He would not only be well cared for here but he would also receive the mental stimulation he needed.

"Jeffey," Beth called. "Time to go."

"Do I have to?" the young boy pleaded. "I'm having too much fun."

"You can come back next week and stay all day while I go to work. Won't that be fun?"

"Yeah," he replied as he obediently followed his mother out the door, giving the playroom one last glance.

Beth's next stop was the Rocky Bluff Crisis Center. It was an eight-block walk from the day care, but fortunately the anticipated storm had not moved in and the walk was invigorating. She shyly pushed open the door and found Dan surrounded by a pile of papers when she walked into the workroom.

Hearing the door open, Dan looked up. "Boy, do I need you!" he chuckled.

"It's always nice to be needed," she replied lightly.

"Take off your coat and stay a while," Dan invited as he rose from his chair. "Can I get you and Jeffey something to drink? A cup of coffee or a soft drink?"

"Thanks, Dan. Don't go to any extra trouble. We can share a coke."

Dan went to the half-size refrigerator and took out a can of pop while Beth and Jeffey made themselves comfortable on the sofa. "Why I stopped by, Dan," Beth began hesitantly, "is to tell you that I just got a full-time job. I'm going to be a clerk-secretary at the high school library."

"Fantastic. When do you begin?"

"Next Monday."

Dan gave a sheepish grin. "Why am I so happy? That means I'm going to lose you as my steady assistant just when you were figuring out my messy system."

"The crisis center did so much for me that I want to be able to help as much as possible," Beth explained. "I was thinking maybe I could stop over for an hour a couple times a week after work and help you out. You sure look overwhelmed now."

"Beth, you're a life saver. I'll be eternally grateful," he snickered.

"Mommy's going to get a car," Jeffey volunteered.

"Good for you," Dan replied as he eyed the mother, amused at the little boy's enthusiasm. "What kind do you want to get?"

"I want to get one like that black fancy one I saw yesterday," Jeffey replied, thinking Dan was talking to him. "But Mom said she'd get me a matchbox car just like it."

Dan roared. "That black Porsche does get around. I think you'll want something a little more conservative."

"And a lot less expensive," Beth echoed.

"I heard that Teresa Lennon was trying to sell her Chevy Capri. Maybe you'd be interested in that," Dan suggested.

"Right now I don't know how I'd pay for it."

"A dollar down and a dollar a month. Maybe if you'd talk to Rick at the bank he'd be able to set up a loan for you now that you have a job."

Beth took a deep breath. "I don't even know how to begin the process. I've never owned a car before and I just got my driver's license a few weeks ago at the college, but I've never had time to do much driving in the drivers' education car."

"I'll give you a hand," Dan promised as he reached for the phone. "Let's call Teresa and see what she wants for her car. Then you can go to the bank with the exact car and price in mind. They'd be more willing to talk to you then."

Dan dialed Teresa Lennon and had an animated conversation with her as he negotiated a price for her eight-year-old car. When he hung up the phone he turned back to Beth. "I think I got the best possible price for this car and she says it's in excellent mechanical condition. Are you still interested?"

"If the payments aren't too high," Beth replied.

Dan reached for his coat. "Then let's go down to the bank and see what they say. I'm parked out back."

Beth's mind spun as Dan and Rick discussed high book values, low book values, and current interest rates. Finally, they settled on a monthly payment schedule. "Does this seem like something you can handle on the salary you'll be making?" the banker asked.

Beth gulped. "Yes, I think so. . . I just don't understand how all of this will work. I haven't even got my first paycheck yet."

"The school has a direct deposit arrangement with this bank. We can do an automatic loan withdrawal from your account the day after your check is deposited so you'll never have to worry about missing a payment," Rick explained as he handed the papers to Beth to sign.

"Sounds too good to be true," she replied as she scanned the forms in front of her. "I'm glad Dan was able to help me get the car. I could never have done it by myself."

❧

Monday morning Beth drove Jeffey to Kinder University

and then parked her car in the faculty parking lot and hurried inside. Viola was already in the office waiting for her. It took over an hour to fill out the necessary paperwork and to explain the benefit package that came with the job. *I didn't realize that Jeffey and I would be covered under a real medical insurance policy,* Beth thought. *I'll no longer have to depend on Medicaid.*

After finishing the paperwork, Beth began her duties in the library. Rebecca Sutherland explained the policies, procedures, and basic routines of the library. By lunchtime Beth was checking out books to the students and helping them with simple questions. *I never dreamed I could ever be helping students in school,* she mused. *I'd always thought school was too difficult for me and I couldn't wait to get away from it.*

⁊⬩

At three o'clock that afternoon Viola Tomkins was standing in the window of the high school office watching the students board the school buses parked along the curb. All the buses had their stop signs extended and red flashing lights on. Suddenly a black Porsche sped past the buses, just missing a couple students who were trying to cross the street.

Viola reached for the phone and dialed the emergency number. "Hello, I'd like to report a black Porsche that was speeding past school busses while they were loading students."

Phil Mooney groaned when Viola's report came in. "That guy in the Porsche really gets around," he said to the dispatcher. "I'm glad I took down his license number earlier. Here," he said to the dispatcher, "fax this to the California Bureau of Motor Vehicles and request information they have on this license number."

Within minutes the return fax was in. The black Porsche was registered to:

> Lance Corporal Mickey Kilmer
> Marine Barracks
> U.S. Naval Station
> San Diego, California

"Hmm. Time to do some more investigative work," Phil said as he read the incoming fax. "What is one of their marines doing here in Rocky Bluff?"

Phil went back to his desk and prepared a request for information about Lance Corporal Mickey Kilmer from the Commanding Officer of the Marine Barracks, U.S. Naval Station, San Diego, California. Soon that fax was also on its way.

"While I'm waiting for a reply I think I'll cruise the streets and see if I can find our offending black Porsche. Montana State Law is very strict about not passing a school bus from either direction while it's loading and unloading passengers," Phil said as he placed his hat on his head and slipped out the door.

Lieutenant Mooney drove past the Sleepy Eye Motel. No black Porsche. He drove past the high school. No black Porsche. No Porsche was found parked in front of any of the fast food restaurants in town. *I guess I struck out this time,* he mused. *I might as well go back to the station and wait for the reply to my fax.*

Phil Mooney was stopped at the door as he entered the station. "The answer to your fax just came in," the dispatcher said as she handed him a sheet of paper.

Phil hurried to his desk and slid into his chair before reading the much awaited fax.

> FAX TO: Chief of Police, Rocky Bluff, MT
> FROM: Commanding Officer, Marine Bar-
>   racks, U.S. Naval Station, San Diego, CA
> REF: Your Request for Info on Kilmer, Mickey
>   (NMI), LCpl. USMC SSAN: 247386225
> Name: Kilmer, Michael (NMI)
> Description: Age: 23 HT: 5'10" WT: 165 lbs.
> Build: Slender   Hair: Brown   Eyes: Hazel
> Complexion: Tan. No identifying marks or scars
> Home of Record: Rte. #2, Box 37,
>   Elders Point, Montana
>
>
> Subject EM tried and convicted by Special Court Martial, this station, for violation of Article 112a UCMJ—Wrongful use, Possession, etc., of Controlled Substances, To Wit: two grams of cocaine.
>
> Subject was sentenced to be reduced to lowest enlisted grade with a forfeiture of all pay and allowances due or to become due and to be dismissed from the United States Marine Corps per Bad Conduct Discharge.
>
> Subject waived appeal and was dropped from the Rolls of USMC 93 days ago.
>   Major Barton Sends

four

"Roy, Dan Blair's on the phone," Edith called, rousing her husband from a nap in his recliner.

"At least the phone is finally for me," he chided good naturedly. "I was beginning to think it was strictly a private line."

"Hello, Dan," Roy greeted as he took the phone from his wife. "How are you doing?"

"I'm okay. More importantly, how have you been doing?"

"To be honest with you, this stupid diabetes has really slowed my body down, but, like I tell Edith, my mind is functioning A-OK but no one will believe me."

Dan chuckled. "I'll believe you, even if no one else will. In fact, that's why I'm calling. I need some advice about the crisis center. Who better to ask than the former director?"

"Why don't you come over and I'll have Edith fix us a cup of coffee," Roy invited. "It's her turn this week to do kitchen duty," he joked.

Edith glared at him across the room and shook her head. She had long since learned that some of his humor was not worth responding to.

A half hour later Roy was offering his guest a cup of coffee. "Dan, I hope you like the coffee. I made it myself. It seems right after I talked to you, Edith had something urgent to tend to which kept her tied up for quite a while. I knew I'd promised you a cup so I went ahead and made it myself."

"The timing was perfect," Edith snickered. "I just can't let him get too dependent on me."

Dan took a sip of his coffee. "I'm glad to see you two haven't lost your sense of humor."

"It's the only thing that's keeping me going," Roy retorted. "Now what great words of wisdom would you like to hear from me?"

"I've noticed an increasing number of non-crisis calls," Dan began. "People seem to be lonely and simply need a sympathetic ear."

"That's a good sign that you've touched a nerve in the community, but it also ties up the phone lines for the true emergencies," Roy replied thoughtfully. "I guess that leaves you with two options."

"What's that?"

"Either you cut all the non-crisis calls short and risk offending the caller, or you can expand your services by putting in more phone lines and recruiting more volunteers," the former director advised.

"But it'll take more than is allotted in my budget to expand, and I don't want to harm the compassionate reputation we've built in the community. I feel like I'm in a catch-twenty-two situation."

"Not necessarily. Why don't you try writing a proposal to the director of United Charities, Barbara Hall, outlining your needs and how you plan to meet those needs? Occasionally they're able to tap other sources and provide emergency assistance for those over budget. However, it'll take a lot of clerical work to write the proposal."

Dan thought a moment. "I know just the person who can help. The problem is she's a mighty busy lady."

"Those are generally the ones who do the best job," Roy reminded him.

≈

Promptly at three forty-five that afternoon Beth Slater breezed into the Rocky Bluff Crisis Center. "Sorry, I'm late. Some students had blocked the faculty parking lot when I went to leave."

Dan glanced at the clock overhead. "I was expecting you at three forty-two, what took you so long?" he teased.

Beth giggled as she hung her coat on the wire framed coat stand. "What's up for today? I can work exactly fifty-eight minutes before I have to pick up Jeffey."

Dan suddenly became serious. "This project could take more than fifty-eight minutes. I'm considering writing a proposal to United Charities for increased funding so we can add more phone lines and volunteers to handle the non-crisis calls."

"That's a great idea," Beth exclaimed as she opened the refrigerator for a soft drink. "There were many times I wanted to call the crisis center when I was lonely and just needed someone to talk to. I was fortunate that Edith Dutton had given me her home phone number so I didn't tie up the crisis lines for the ones who really needed it."

"But that means a lot of typing," Dan warned her.

"I'm up to it," Beth assured him. "I could talk to the computer lab teacher and maybe he'd let me take one of the older computers home for the weekend to work on this project."

"Beth, you're an absolute dear. I'm sure you'll have a lot of extra stars in your crown when you get to Glory for taking on this project," the director of the center teased.

Beth helped Dan outline what he wanted to say in the proposal and then hurried to Kinder University.

"Hi, Mommy," Jeffey shouted as his mother entered the playroom. "Do you want to see the pictures I drew today?"

Jeffey took his mother's hand and proudly led her to the table in the corner. "The fancy black car kept driving past our school while I was outside for recess so I decided to draw some pictures of it. They're pretty good, aren't they?"

Cold chills traveled down Beth's spine. *What is Jeffey's fascination with that car?* she thought. *That car seems to be every place and yet it's never close enough to see the driver.*

❧

A fresh blanket of snow covered Rocky Bluff when Beth left for work the next morning. The biting cold dampened her spirits and the fear of her first drive on snow-packed streets enveloped her. A sense of apprehension tried to smother her, but she took a deep breath. *I'm a working woman now. I'm only experiencing what every other Montana woman is facing this morning. With God's help I can handle it.*

Beth eased the car slowly toward Kinder University. Jeffey was eager to play with his new friends. However, this was the first time it was hard for Beth to say 'Goodbye'. *I'm merely suffering from separation anxiety,* she tried to console herself.

The grayness of the skies echoed Beth's spirit. She tried to keep a smile pasted on her face while she checked out books to students and shelved those they returned. As she was walking down the hall from lunch, Grady Walker approached her with a grim look on his face. "Beth, would you come into my office please."

Panic raced through her as she followed her principal down the hall like a disobedient student. *Have I done something wrong? Aren't they happy with my work here? I just bought my car, I can't afford to be fired now.*

Mr. Walker motioned for her to enter his office and then

he closed the door behind him. Terror gripped her as she saw Lieutenant Mooney and Sergeant Packwood standing there.

"Beth, won't you sit down," Mr. Walker said, as he pointed to the same table and chairs she sat in during her interview two weeks before.

"Beth, I have some bad new for you," Phil Mooney began. "Jeffey has disappeared from Kinder University Day Care."

The young mother sat in stunned silence. She wanted to scream but her mouth froze shut. Finally, she was able to whisper. "You must be mistaken. Jeffey loved it there. He would never run away."

"We don't think he ran away," Sergeant Packwood tried to explain.

Beth began sobbing hysterically. "Then what happened to my baby?"

"At this time all we know is what the directors and teachers have told us. The teacher was outside with eight children when one of them fell on the ice and received what she thought may have been a concussion. After taking care of the injured child, she returned to the others but Jeffey was missing. There were small footprints in the snow up to the fence, large men's boot prints on the other side of the fence, and tire marks near the sidewalk. The police are now trying to identify the kind of car by the type of tires."

Beth continued sobbing while the three men sat there in tense silence. Nothing would be able to take away her pain until her child was in her arms. Her baby was gone.

Finally, Mr. Walker put his hand on Beth's shoulder. "Beth, is there somewhere you'd like to go? I'll drive you there myself. Your car will be all right in the faculty parking lot overnight."

"I want to see Edith Dutton," Beth mumbled between sobs.

Mr. Walker had his secretary go to the library and get Beth's coat and purse. He then told Viola to call Edith Dutton and tell her they were on their way and they would explain the circumstances when they got there.

"If we have any developments we'll be in touch with you either at Mrs. Dutton's or at your home," Lieutenant Mooney explained softly. "Do try to get some rest. You'll need all the strength you can muster."

Numb with shock, Beth scarcely felt the cold biting wind that blew across the faculty parking lot. Grady gently directed her to the principal's parking stall. She sobbed softly as he drove on the snow-packed streets to the Dutton residence.

Mr. Walker escorted Beth to the door and rang the bell. "Do come in out of the cold," Edith invited, as she observed the distraught young woman before her. "What has happened?"

"Jeffey disappeared from Kinder University," Grady Walker explained. "It looks like a kidnapping."

Edith's face blanched as she wrapped her arms around Beth to comfort her. "How can that be? They take such good care of the children there."

"One of the new teachers took the older children outside for a few minutes to play in the snow," Grady explained. "One of them slipped on the ice and hurt his head. While her attention was directed to him, Jeffey vanished."

"Do they have any idea who did it?" Roy asked as he straightened himself up in his recliner.

"Lieutenant Mooney said the leads are pretty slim now, but they're doing all they can." The principal turned his attention back to the stunned mother. "I need to get back to school now, but if there's anything I can do don't hesitate to ask. We'll give you a few days personal leave until Jeffey is found."

"Thank you for all you've done," Beth muttered as she slowly regained her composure.

"Beth, let me hang up your coat," Edith said gently. "Why don't you stretch out on the sofa and rest while I make some herb tea. That always seems to have a soothing effect for me."

As Edith walked to the kitchen the phone rang.

"Hello."

"Hello, Edith," a worried voice greeted. "This is Sonya Turner. Does Beth Slater happen to be at your house? I called the school and whoever answered the phone said she left with Mr. Walker."

"Yes, she is. Would you like to speak to her?"

"If it's okay with you, I'd rather see her in person," Sonya replied.

"I'm sure that would mean a lot to her. Do stop over," Edith invited. "I'm just putting on a pot of herb tea now."

Within minutes, Edith, Beth, and Sonya sat glumly in the Dutton's living room sipping herb tea while Roy reclined restlessly in his chair, unable to comfort the grieving women.

"Beth, you don't know how sorry I am about this," Sonya said with tears in her eyes. "If only we hadn't let the children go out and play in the snow today, this wouldn't have happened."

"I didn't think anything like this would happen in Rocky Bluff," Beth muttered. "Occasionally we hear of something happening in Billings, but never here. And why Jeffey? He's such a sweet loving child."

Sonya bit her lip. "I just don't understand," she confided. "I know the police are doing all they can. They worked quite a while in front of the day care. Scott Packwood said they're going to make plaster models of the foot and tire imprints in the snow and send them to the crime lab in Missoula. Hopefully, that'll give them a lead."

"I just don't see how anyone could do such a thing to an innocent child," Beth muttered as she tried to hold back her tears. "Don't they have any human decency?"

"I hope they catch the guy, lock him up, and throw away the key," Roy said, unable to hide his anger.

The women each nodded in agreement.

"I wish I could stay longer," Sonya said as she stood to leave. "But I need to get back to the center so others can take their break. If you hear any word on Jeffey, would you let me know? We'll all be praying for him."

"Thanks," Beth mumbled, as Sonya slipped quietly out the front door.

Beth stretched out on the sofa and pulled the afghan over her. Nothing could remove the cold chill that encased her except the warm embrace of her son. She wanted to slip into unconsciousness, but sleep avoided her as memories of Jeffey laughing and playing danced before her.

A cloud of gloom hung over the Dutton's home. An hour later the silence was broken by the ringing of the doorbell. "I hope that's the police with some word on Jeffey," Roy exclaimed as he went to answer the door.

Roy was unable to hide his disappointment. "It's Dan," he announced, motioning for him to come in.

"Don't sound so unhappy with my arrival," Dan said, trying to ease the tension.

"I'm sorry," Roy apologized. "We were just hoping it was the police with some word about Jeffey."

The director of the crisis center forced a faint smile. "That's okay. I just came by to see how Beth was doing." He walked across the room and took her hand.

"I'm doing terrible," she said as she sat up so he could join her on the sofa. "I just want my baby back."

"The police are doing all they can." Dan squeezed her hand tighter. "I'm sure Jeffey has an entire legion of guardian angels taking care of him right now."

"I hope you're right," Beth replied. She sat in silence for a moment before she spoke. Then turning to her friend she said, "Dan, would you mind giving me a ride home? My car is still in the school parking lot. I want to be home in case the police call with any word on Jeffey."

"Sure," Dan replied as he rose from the sofa. "Let me get your coat. I'll take you home and then walk over to the school and get your car for you. While I'm doing that, would you mind ordering out for pizza?"

"Food is the last thing on my mind," Beth replied as she slipped into her coat. "But I guess it's getting about that time."

"Time is getting away from us," Edith reminded her. "You need to keep up your strength for when Jeffey comes home."

"When I get home I should call my parents in Glasgow," Beth sighed. "They disowned me when I got pregnant with Jeffey, but I suppose it'll be on all the evening news broadcasts tonight so they probably should hear it first from me."

"I know calling your folks will be difficult, but I'll be by your side to give you moral support," Dan encouraged as they walked to his car parked in the drive.

"I'm sure they'll tell me, 'I knew you couldn't handle that baby by yourself. You should have had an abortion like we wanted you to'," Beth sighed as she choked back the tears. "Can you imagine having aborted little Jeffey? He's the most precious child there ever could be."

When Beth opened the door to her apartment she burst into hysterical sobs once again as Dan held her gently in his arms. Jeffey's favorite stuffed toy was on the chair. His artwork covered the refrigerator and his inflatable chair was still in front of the TV where he left it that morning. Just as her tears began to subside and her body relaxed, the doorbell rang.

"I hope that's the police with word about Jeffey," she said, as Dan answered the door.

"Hello, Pastor Rhodes," Dan greeted.

"Is Beth home? I just heard what happened to Jeffey and I wanted to stop and see how she was doing," Pastor Rhodes said as he stomped the snow from his shoes and entered the cozy apartment.

"Things are plenty tough," Beth admitted as the pastor took the chair next to the sofa.

"I imagine they are," he acknowledged. "We just have to trust that Jeffey's in God's hands right now and He is protecting him from all harm. The church prayer chain is praying for him right now and will continue to do so until he's returned."

"Thanks for your support," Beth replied as she glanced at the clock overhead. "It's time for the five-thirty news. I want to see if they have any news about Jeffey."

Dan took the remote and clicked on channel five just as the theme song of the news broadcast began. Sure enough the lead story was: CHILD SNATCHED FROM LOCAL DAY CARE. Beth's eyes filled with tears as she listened to the newscaster rehash the events of the day. They ended with a picture of Jeffey that was taken the first day at Kinder

University. The public was asked that if they had any knowledge as to the whereabouts of the child to please call the Rocky Bluff Police Department.

After the evening news Pastor Rhodes led the worried mother in a prayer of protection for her child, and comfort and strength for herself.

Beth felt more at peace as she closed the door behind her pastor. "I don't know what I'd do without the love and support everyone has shown me," she said to Dan as she squeezed his hand. She then took a deep breath. "Now I have to call my parents. I hope they didn't see the news, but I think they can get this channel on cable in Glasgow now."

Beth checked her address book and dialed the long-forgotten number.

"Hello, Mother," she greeted as a familiar voice answered the phone. "This is Beth."

"Honey, how are you? We've been so worried about you, not knowing where you've been for so many years," Mrs. Slater said as she choked back her tears.

"Mom, something terrible has happened," Beth sobbed.

"We know. We just saw your baby's picture on the evening news. He's a beautiful child. Your dad and I are going to leave first thing in the morning to come to Rocky Bluff and help with the search for him. We love you, darling."

"Mom, you haven't said that since I was a little girl," Beth sobbed.

"I'm sorry," Mrs. Slater admitted. "But those times are over. We want to be a family again with our beautiful grandson. Will you please forgive us for not standing behind you when you needed us the most?"

"Of course," Beth assured them with tears streaming down her cheeks. "I need you more then ever right now."

five

"Where are you taking me?" Jeffey cried as the black Porsche sped away from Kinder University.

"I thought you'd like to ride in my new car," the stranger replied. "Only extra special people get to ride in this car. Do you like it?"

The child leaned back in the seat and relaxed. "Yeah, it's neat. I have a matchbox car just like it."

Jeffey sat in awe as the Porsche reached the outskirts of Rocky Bluff. His dream of being in a fancy car had come true.

"Do you want to see how fast the car can go, just like in the races?" the driver asked.

"Yeah, that'd be fun," Jeffey shouted excitedly. "I've never been to the races but I've seen them on TV."

The black Porsche raced west toward Great Falls. Occasionally, it slid on the icy snow-packed pavement, but the driver immediately regained control and regained speed.

"Jeffey, do you know who I am?"

"No, but you have a neat car," the child innocently replied.

"I'm your daddy."

"I don't have a daddy," Jeffey stated in a matter of fact tone. "It's just me and my Mommy."

"She didn't tell you about me because I was in the Marines."

"You mean you were a real GI Joe?"

Mickey Kilmer laughed. "Something like that. Now that I'm out, you and I can do a lot of fun things together."

"But what about Mommy?"

"She has a new job. Wouldn't you rather ride in my car than go to day care every day?"

Jeffey thought for a moment. "I guess so. But I like Kinder University. It's fun."

The warmth in the car heater made Jeffey sleepy and he laid his head against the back of the seat and went to sleep. The highway became more snow-packed and slippery with each passing mile. Mickey was forced to decrease his speed just to stay on the road. The miles passed slowly for him.

Ten miles out of Great Falls, Mickey awakened the sleeping child. "Jeffey, we're going to stop here. I need to get some snow tires. The roads are just too slick to drive on. If anyone asks you, tell them we're on our way to see your grandma."

"But I don't have a grandma," Jeffey protested. "Except for my Granny Edith."

"You'll be meeting all kinds of new people," Mickey explained, trying to calm the child's fears so he would not alert a passerby. "Until today you didn't know you had a daddy and now we're the best of friends. Right?"

"Yeah, I guess so," he replied doubtfully.

Mickey turned his car into the first Tire Shop he came to on Tenth Avenue South—Don's Tire and Rubber. "Wait here a minute while I see if they have what I need," he directed the child.

Mickey got out of the car and hurried into the sales shop. "Do you have any snow tires to fit my Porsche?" he demanded of a nearby salesman.

"Pretty fancy car to be driving on these kind of roads," the salesman commented as he looked out the plate glass window. "I'll have to check the computer to see if we have any that are compatible. It's not very common in Montana."

Mickey nervously watched the traffic while the salesman punched the keys of the computer. He stood motionless as a Great Falls Police Car stopped at the corner light.

The salesman looked up from the computer screen. "Looks like you're in luck," he assured Mickey. "We still have two left, but we have such a backlog because of this storm we won't have time to get to them until tomorrow."

"But I have to get on the road as soon as possible," Mickey pleaded. "My mother is critically ill and my father asked me to come home right away. If I don't get home tonight I may not get to say 'good-bye'."

The salesman stroked his chin. "Hmm. If that's the case, maybe we'll be able to slip you in right now. It'll probably take us about an hour and a half if you want to go and get something to eat."

We Montanans are so naive we'd believe any hard luck story, Mickey snickered as he walked back to his car. "Come on, Son," he said loud enough for the salesman to hear. "Time to get something to eat before we go on to grandma's house."

❧

After hanging up from talking with her mother, Beth Slater paced nervously around her small apartment. "Beth, why don't you sit down and try to watch television with me? You're only wearing yourself out by pacing."

"I wonder if the police have any new leads?" Beth said as she peered into the night blackness. "Statistics say that the longer a child is missing the less likely you are to get him back at all," she sighed.

"Why don't you call the police station and find out,"

Dan suggested.

Beth dialed the non-emergency police number. "Hello, is Lieutenant Mooney there please?" she asked the receptionist. "This is Beth Slater."

"One moment please."

The silence on the line was nearly deafening before a deep voice answered. "Hello, Beth. This is Lieutenant Mooney. How are you doing?"

"I'm plenty worried. Have there been any developments?"

"We probably won't know anything until morning," Phil explained. "Scott caught the last Treasure State plane to Missoula this afternoon to hand carry the plaster modes of the footprints and the tire print to the crime lab. He's supposed to call me first thing in the morning with results. I don't think we'll know anything until then. But I'll let you know as soon as I hear anything."

"Thanks," she muttered as she hung up the phone.

"No more news," Beth sighed as she turned her attention back to Dan.

"Say, we forgot all about the pizza we were going to order. What kind do you like?" Dan said, trying to ease her troubled mind.

"Jeffey and I usually have Canadian Bacon," she replied.

"That sounds good. Now how about you calling the Pizza Palace and placing the order? If you'll give me the keys to your car, I'll walk over to the school and drive it back. If they guarantee thirty-minute delivery, I should be back long before the pizza gets here."

Beth reached for her purse and handed Dan her keys. He slipped out the door into the night blackness while she took out the phone directory and searched the yellow pages under P.

A string of friends and well-wishers either came to Beth's apartment or called that evening. Dan remained constantly by her side helping her tell the story of Jeffey's disappearance over and over again. By ten o'clock the last of the guests left and Beth and Dan turned on the ten o'clock news. Again Jeffey was the lead story.

"Flashing his picture all across the state on TV, someone's sure to recognize him," Beth sighed as the same picture of him appeared on the screen.

"I'm sure we'll have some good news in the morning when Scott calls from the crime lab," Dan assured her as he patted her hand and stood to leave. "Now why don't you go to bed and try to get some rest? I'll call you first thing in the morning."

&

Eight o'clock the next morning Dan was knocking at Beth's door with a sack of groceries. "I thought I'd make you one of my specialties for breakfast," he grinned when she opened the door dressed in a crumpled sweat suit. "How does a Denver omelet sound?"

"I appreciate your efforts," Beth sighed as she motioned for him to enter. "I'm just not in the eating mood. I don't think I slept a bit all night."

"That's all the more reason to have a hearty breakfast."

Within thirty minutes Dan had a lavish breakfast on the table. Beth did her best to compliment him on his cooking, but every bite laid flat in her mouth. When they finished, Dan insisted on doing the dishes alone so she could get some of the rest she missed during the long night.

Beth's state of semiconsciousness was broken with the ring of the door bell. Dan hurried to answer it.

"Phil, do come in. I hope you have some good news for

us," he said as he swung the door open and then stepped aside.

"Let's just say I have some interesting news," the officer responded as he headed for an overstuffed chair beside the sofa where Beth was resting. "Scott just called from the crime lab in Missoula. They found that the car tracks were made by a Pirelli radial tire size two fifty-five forty Z R seventeen. This particular tire is manufactured by Pirelli Tire Company in Italy. It's standard equipment on all model Nine Eleven Porches. The boot print was made by a size ten army issue style combat boot. The weight of the wearer is estimated between one hundred and fifty-five and one hundred and seventy-five."

"Well, at least that's a beginning," Dan replied. "Not too many people in Rocky Bluff drive a Porsche."

"How about that black Porsche that's been cruising around town for the last week or so?" Beth asked. "Who does that belong to?"

"Interesting enough, we just ran a make on it the day before yesterday when the driver failed to stop for the school buses that were loading students," Lieutenant Mooney explained. "We traced it to a Mickey Kilmer who was kicked out of the marine corps with a Bad Conduct Discharge about three months ago for possession of cocaine."

Beth gasped and turned ashen.

"Do you know him?" Dan and Phil asked in unison.

"He's Jeffey's father. I haven't seen him since I told him I was three months pregnant."

Lieutenant Mooney tried not to display his shock. "We've placed an All Points Bulletin out for his arrest," he explained matter-of-factly. "I'm sure we'll have your baby back in a few days. I better get back to the station in case we have any response to our APB."

After the police officer left, Beth turned to Dan. "Would you mind driving me to Edith's? I want to bring her up on the latest developments but I don't feel up to driving on these slick streets."

"I'd be delighted to," Dan said as he reached for his coat. "Get your coat."

As they turned the corner toward the Dutton residence they could scarcely believe their eyes. Cars lined both sides of the street. "They all seem to be at the Dutton's. I hope they're both okay," Beth said, trying to mask her sense of panic.

"I haven't heard an ambulance siren this morning so I assume that they are," Dan assured her.

When Beth entered the Dutton's living room she found herself surrounded by hugs and well-wishers. "We're in the process of organizing a Bring Jeffy Home Committee," Edith explained as she helped Beth off with her coat. "We have a number of ideas that we're working on."

What do you think of this as a Missing Child Poster?" Teresa Lennon asked as she held up a neatly-printed poster with Jeffey's enlarged photograph in the center.

Tears welled in her eyes as she surveyed the notice with Jeffey's picture, description, and the phone number of the Rocky Bluff Police Department. "It's perfect," she murmured. "I don't know what to say."

"If you like it, Teresa said she'd take it over to the print shop and have ten thousand copies made," Edith explained as she patted the frightened mother on the shoulder.

"But I don't make enough money to pay for it," Beth said meekly.

"We'll worry about the financing," Edith assured her.

"We have already begun placing jugs in all the stores to help meet expenses."

"The president of the bank has already set up a Jeffey Slater account and he donated the first one hundred dollars," Teresa exclaimed excitedly.

Beth shook her head in amazement. "I can't believe everyone is doing this for me."

"We're doing it for both you and Jeffey," Patricia Reagan replied as she hugged her friend. "We love you both."

Teresa Lennon, the Director of the Spouse Abuse Center, was obviously one of the leaders of the ad hoc committee. "We've also contacted several dairies that distribute milk in schools in the Northwestern United States and Canada," she explained as she laid her poster aside. "They've agreed to print Jeffey's picture on the Missing Children's milk cartons. Someone's bound to recognize him."

"Canada?" Beth questioned. "Do you really think he could have gone up there?"

"Anything's possible," Teresa replied. "The border is only two hundred miles away. It's a mighty long border, with a lot of crossings between Montana and Canada."

"We're in the process of listing US and Canadian Agencies to notify and provide them a copy of the poster," Edith went on to explain. "I'm sure we'll need more than ten thousand, but that's a good starting number."

"That's not all we're doing," Larry Reynolds added. "I've gotten fairly efficient with the computer since I started working at Harkness Hardware Store. I've placed Jeffey's picture in an On-line Database of Missing Children that's available to all computer enthusiasts, social services, and law enforcement agencies. Perhaps someone will recognize him there."

"You've all been so kind," Beth said. "Even my parents are coming from Glasgow to help look for Jeffey."

A look of shock spread across Edith's face. "I thought they had disowned you when you got pregnant and didn't get an abortion."

"They did," Beth replied. "But I called them as soon as the news was on TV. When they saw Jeffey's picture on TV last night they said they felt terrible about the way they acted toward me. They want to get to know the grandson that might not have been if I had listened to them and had an abortion."

"I wonder if they'll be able to travel from town to town, truck stop to truck stop hanging Jeffey's posters," Edith pondered. "Most of us aren't able to get away from our families and jobs for very long and Montana has a lot of territory to cover."

"I imagine Dad would like to do that," Beth responded thoughtfully. "He used to be an over-the-road trucker and knows all their hangouts. He's really missed the road since he retired. They should arrive late this afternoon and we can ask them then."

The ringing of the phone interrupted the enthusiastic plans being made.

Edith hurried to the phone. "Hello."

"Hello, Edith. This is Phil Mooney. Does Beth Slater happen to be there? I checked her apartment and no one was there."

"Yes, she is," Edith chuckled. "Along with half the town of Rocky Bluff. Just a moment and I'll put her on."

The entire group went silent as Beth took the phone.

"Beth, I just got our first response to our All Points Bulletin."

Beth's eyes lit up. "What was it?"

"The police department in Great Falls just called and said they did see a black Porsche about five p.m. yesterday getting snow tires at Don's Tire and Rubber on Tenth Avenue South," Lieutenant Mooney explained.

"Were they sure it was Mickey?"

"They're pretty confident," Phil assured her. "When they talked with the salesman at Don's Tire they said that the driver fit Mickey Kilmer's description and he was traveling with a small boy. He gave them some story that he was on his way home to see his ailing mother."

"But Mickey's mother lives in Elders Point," Beth protested. "That's in the far southeastern part of the state. He's going the wrong direction."

"Don't worry. We're contacting all the border crossing stations to make sure he doesn't enter Canada. It'll be a lot harder to locate Jeffey if Mickey does cross the Canadian border," Phil could scarcely hide the frustration in his voice. "Let's hope he kept going west or turned south from there."

Beth hung up the phone and turned to the group. "That was Lieutenant Mooney from the police department. He came by my place earlier today and told me that the car tracks found where Jeffey was kidnapped belonged to that black Porsche that has been seen all over town. The Porsche belongs to Mickey Kilmer, who was kicked out of the Marine Corps three months ago." She hesitated as all eyes remained glued on her in astonishment. "Mickey is Jeffey's father," Beth took another deep breath. "Lieutenant Mooney said that the Great Falls police just called and that Mickey and Jeffey were spotted in Great Falls about five p.m. yesterday."

With that Beth collapsed to the floor. Dan was immediately kneeling beside. "Are you okay?" he whispered.

"I'm sorry," she murmured. "I'm so tired I guess I can't keep my body functioning."

"I'll take you home where you can rest," Dan said, helping her to her feet. "The Bring Jeffy Home Committee is in good hands."

Dan took Beth home where she immediately flopped on her sofa. He gently covered her with an afghan and sat down in the chair to read the morning newspaper. Of course, the disappearance of Jeffey Slater was headline news. Dan dozed off himself, but was soon awakened by the door bell.

"Scott, you're back from Missoula already," Dan said as he opened the door.

"I took the next Treasure State flight home. We don't have any time to lose in finding Jeffey," he explained. "I just wanted to stop by and see how Beth was doing."

"She's holding up fairly well," Dan assured him. "But she's extremely tired. She didn't get much rest last night."

"I can imagine," Scott sympathized. "When she wakes up would you tell her that a border guard outside Sweetgrass just called and said that a man driving a black Porsche with a young boy sleeping in the back seat crossed the border just before midnight last night. He said the driver appeared so distraught about getting home to his ailing mother that he did not detain him."

"Oh, no," Dan sighed. "Only a miracle will get him home now."

six

"Mr. Walker, thanks for letting me have a few days off work after Jeffey was kidnapped," Beth Slater said as she entered his office the week after her child had disappeared. "I just can't stay alone in that apartment waiting and watching, wondering if he'll ever come back. Even my parents returned to Glasgow until we get word on his whereabouts. At least I can try to earn a little to help pay for his search."

"I'm glad you're back," Grady Walker said as he rose from his chair. "I know Rebecca Sutherland really missed you."

"I'm sure she's way behind in her clerical work. I'll try to help her get caught up as fast as possible."

Beth had trouble smiling at the students as she checked out books and reshelved the returned ones. Many teachers and school personnel stopped to encourage her, but nothing would take away the pain of seeing the many posters with her giggling son's face. Still school was better than sitting alone in her apartment waiting.

At three-thirty Beth dreaded going home. She drove aimlessly downtown and parked her car in front of the crisis center. Her shoulders drooped as she walked into the center.

"How was your first day back at work?" Dan asked as he surveyed her lined face.

"All I can say is that I survived another day without Jeffey," she muttered as she took her coat off and hung it on the coat rack. "I hope he'll be home for Thanksgiving."

"You're doing a great job hanging in there," Dan said. "Have you had any news today?"

"I'm afraid not. Everything's at a standstill. Do you have any clerical work you'd like to have done? I need to do something to keep my mind busy. When I think about Jeffey I nearly go crazy."

"I still haven't typed the proposal for additional funding for the crisis center. Would you like to work on that?" he asked as he took a manila folder from the cabinet beside his desk.

"Sure. Maybe something good will come out of it."

"Beth, do you know Jean Thompson, Edith's daughter?"

"Yes, I met her at the Harkness Hardware Store Grand Reopening after their big fire. Edith talks about her a lot. Jean's daughter is just a few months younger than Jeffey."

"Did you know that she and her husband moved to Running Butte to open another hardware store?" Dan queried as he joined Beth on the sofa.

Beth nodded her head in agreement. "I'd heard that. Edith was real excited about them coming back to Montana."

"Anyway while her husband is busy getting the hardware store set up, Jean is head-over-heels trying to get a medical clinic started for the Indians. That tribe has been neglected by the government for a long time."

"Jean would be good at that," Beth smiled. "They say she did a fantastic job at the Chamberlain Hospital and they hated to lose her."

Dan propped his feet on the ottoman and grinned. "Jean called this morning and asked if I could come for lunch

Saturday and bring Roy and Edith along. She wants to start a crisis center similar to what we have in Rocky Bluff only on a smaller scale."

"That sounds like a great idea," Beth responded. "You know what I think of the necessity of crisis lines. I don't know where I'd be if Rocky Bluff hadn't had one when I needed help."

"Jean said she needed all the help she could get from the experts in the field. Imagine me an expert at anything," Dan snickered.

A smile spread across Beth's tense face. "Anyone who can do what you do is an expert. Not everyone can look at other people's problems as compassionately and objectively as you do."

Dan reached for her hand. "Flattery will get you everywhere," he replied light-heartedly. "She also wondered if you could come along. She knows you're one of our strongest supporters."

"I can't plan anything until Jeffey is home," Beth replied. "Everything is hour by hour."

"If there's any news on Jeffey I'm sure none of us will want to go. We'll just call and reschedule."

"It sounds good to me. I'll let Lieutenant Mooney know where I'll be so he can call me there if there are any new developments."

Beth remained at the crisis center and typed on the proposal until five o'clock and then hurried home to watch the evening news. The disappearance of Jeffey was no longer the lead story but occasionally someone came up with a new theory and got a little media time. The evening news was the same as nearly every other day: Tribal warfare in Africa, corruption in Washington, and another Speedy Mart was held up in Billings.

The following day at work went better for Beth. The pain was still there but her smile for the students came a little more naturally. At three-thirty she drove directly to her apartment complex and parked her car in the stall. She hurried to the boxes on the curb to get her mail. Usually she only got "Current Occupant" mail but today she discovered a business envelope with no return address. The postmark was smudged, but it looked like it was mailed within the state.

This is different, she mused. *Usually the envelopes I get say "TO THE LUCKY WINNER: please send money to collect your prize."*

Beth unlocked her door and stepped inside. The letter was typed on cheap, plain paper using an old-fashion typewriter whose ribbon had seen many miles.

> *To: Beth Slater*
>
> *I saw your baby Jeffey's picture on television. He's an adorable child. He does not deserve to grow up with an unwed teenage mother living off welfare. Our tax money does not need to support the likes of you. Women with low morals should not be allowed to keep their babies. Your child is better off with his natural father who would be willing to work and earn a salary and not live off welfare the way you do.*
>
> *You should clean up your life, get a job and don't spread any diseases.*
>
>

Signed,

A Concerned Citizen

Beth stood in stunned silence and then burst into tears. She took her keys from her purse, locked the door behind her, and ran to her car. She could hardly see through her tear-filled eyes as she drove toward Edith Dutton's home. Parking her car in the drive, she raced toward the front door.

"Beth's, what's happened?" Edith asked as the young woman fell into her arms sobbing.

Beth reached into her coat pocket and took out the crumpled envelope. "This came in the mail today. I don't even know how they got my address."

"The phone book is easy enough," Edith replied as the pair sat down together on Edith's living room sofa. A scowl spread across Edith's face as she read the offending letter.

Edith shook her head in disgust. "This person is full of hate. We needn't concern ourselves with this garbage. He, or she, doesn't even have the facts straight. You're an excellent mother," Edith assured her. "You know you don't have loose morals. You know you used the welfare system the right way—you used it to support your baby while you got an education so you could support both of you. You also know that it's the baby's father who has the question-able morals."

"Does everyone think this of me?" Beth sobbed.

"Of course not, honey," Edith comforted. "However, there are all kinds of kooks out there. That's why Jeffey is not with you right now."

"I really tried to be a good mother," Beth continued to sob. "I know it was wrong that I got pregnant in the first place, but that was such a long time ago. Will I be con-demned all my life for that? Is that why God let Jeffey be taken away from me?"

"Beth, Jesus died on the cross for your sins along with everyone else's. God didn't let Jeffey be taken from you because of your sin. Jeffey was taken because Mickey is acting very irresponsibly."

"Pastor Rhodes explained that to me a long time ago," the distraught woman confided, "but sometimes I still feel guilty even if my affair with Mickey happened five years ago. I'm afraid people will always look down on me."

"The writer of this letter has not walked in your shoes. He or she doesn't understand what you've been through," Edith tried to explain. "He's the one that should be pitied. He must have an awfully miserable life to be filled with this much hate."

"I don't think I'll ever get this letter out of my mind," Beth whispered. "It hurts so deeply."

"Let's turn it over to Lieutenant Mooney to add to Jeffey's file. That way you'll never be tempted to go back and reread it. Who knows, maybe the sender had something to do with Mickey." Edith went to the phone and dialed the local police station. Beth did not need anything else to torture her troubled mind.

❧

Constable Gene Hanson parked his Royal Canadian Mounted Police cruiser in the West Elementary School visitor's spot. Law Enforcement Day in the Calgary Schools was one of his favorite assignments. He spent the entire day going from class to class teaching the children about safety and law protection. He had time to meet one-on-one with them during recess and he especially enjoyed eating lunch in the noisy cafeteria.

At eleven forty-five the mountie found himself surrounded

by twelve third graders complaining about their hot dogs while they enjoyed every bite. "Do you know why these kids' pictures are on the milk cartons?" he asked the freckled-faced redhead across from him.

"Yeah, I think they got kidnapped, or something," he responded matter-of-factly. "We're suppose to watch for them and then call the police if we see them."

"You learned your lesson well," Constable Hanson replied.

"Look at this little kid," the petite brunette next to him said. "His name is Jeffey Slater. He sure is cute. We drove through Rocky Bluff, Montana, last summer on vacation. I wonder if we saw the kidnapper and didn't know it."

"You can never tell a kidnapper by just looking at them," the Constable Hanson explained. "Sometimes they'll even try to be your best friend."

"What are you going to do when you leave the school?" a pudgy boy queried.

"I'll probably go catch a speeder or a motorist who ran a stop sign," he responded lightheartedly. "All the vacationers have left, so business is pretty slow this time of year."

૨ଉ

That afternoon while Gene Hanson and his partner Kenneth Hogan were on routine patrol they noticed a black Porsche speeding down Main Street as they approached the intersection. Gene immediately turned on his red lights and siren, and gave pursuit.

"Can we get close enough to read the plates," Constable Hogan asked.

"The traffic is so heavy I'm afraid we'll endanger someone

if I go any faster," Gene replied as his knuckles gripped tighter around the steering wheel. "We're already going sixty-five kilometers in a thirty-five zone and he's pulling away from us. We better radio ahead for someone to block his path."

Ten blocks further down the street near the outskirts of town two more police cruisers joined the chase and the three of them forced the black Porsche into a used car lot. Constable Hanson approached the car where the other mounties had the driver spread-eagled against the side of the Porsche. A frightened child whimpered in the front seat. Seeing that his colleagues had the situation well in hand, he turned his attention to the child.

"Hi, what's your name?" Constable Hanson asked.

"Jeffey."

Suddenly the face on the carton at lunch flashed before him. "Is your last name Slater?"

"Yeah," he mumbled in amazement. "How'd you know?"

"You're a pretty famous guy," Constable Hanson reminded him. "I bet you're even from Rocky Bluff, Montana."

"Wow, you're good."

Constable Hogan joined the arresting constables. "I just ran a computer check on that California license plate and there is an All Points Bulletin on it from the state of Montana for kidnapping."

"I didn't do anything," Mickey snarled. "He's my own kid."

"We'll have to check into that," Constable Hogan replied firmly. "First we'll need to inspect your car." Kenneth opened up the front door of the Porsche and began looking around. Under the front seat was a small brown box. He opened it to find a fine white powder. He put it to his nose and then rubbed a few particles between his fingers.

"Looks like we have a couple a kilos of cocaine here, boys," he said as he handed the box to Constable Hanson. Kenneth Hogan continued in his search. Inside the glove compartment he found a small handgun. He checked the trunk, but it contained only a set of tools and a man's suitcase full of clothing.

"I've finished the search," Constable Hogan stated. "Let's take him in. You guys can have Mickey and we'll take the child. I'll call for a tow truck to bring the Porsche down to headquarters."

Jeffey sat in the back seat of the police car with his eyes wide and frightened. On the one hand he was excited about getting to ride in the police car, but on the other hand he was frightened seeing the man who claimed he was his daddy being arrested. "Where are we going?" he cried. "I want my mommy."

♨

Nine o'clock that night Lieutenant Phil Mooney was finishing the daily paperwork at Rocky Bluff Police Station when the phone on his desk buzzed.

"Phil, a Constable Hanson from the Canadian Mounties would like to speak with you," the night dispatcher said as he picked up the phone.

Phil pushed the red flashing button on his phone. "Hello, this is Lieutenant Mooney."

"Lieutenant Mooney, in response to your APB we have arrested Mickey Kilmer. The child Jeffey Slater was with him. However, we found two kilos of cocaine and a handgun in his possession so we will be having plans for him for a long while."

"How is the child?" Lieutenant Mooney asked.

"He's fine, but extremely frightened," Gene Hanson replied. "He keeps asking for his mother. We've put him in protective custody until we can get this sorted out. With the laws of two countries involved, both the mother and the father are going to need a couple good attorneys."

"I'll let the mother know right away that the child is safe."

"Would you have her get an attorney right away? We'll be calling first thing in the morning with arrangements from this end," Constable Hanson explained.

"Would you have all of your legal contacts go through our Little Big Horn County Attorney Stuart Leonard?" Lieutenant Mooney asked. "He's already on top of the case and will do a fine job. Thanks for calling. We'll be in touch tomorrow."

All the employees in the police station burst into an excited cheer when they heard that Jeffey had been located.

"Come on, Scott, let's go tell Beth," Phil said as he motioned toward his partner.

Beth sat in front of the TV mindlessly watching the images flicker across the screen. She was scarcely aware when one show ended and another began. She was brought back to reality with the ringing of her doorbell. Cautiously, she opened the door and saw the two police officers standing there. Unlatching the chain, she invited them in.

"Did they find Jeffey?" she pleaded as she observed the broad smiles on both their faces.

Phil smiled "He's in protective custody in Calgary, Alberta, Canada."

Beth gave a shout for joy and spontaneously hugged each

of them. "Is he all right?"

Phil placed a hand on her shoulder. "They say he's fine, just a little frightened. He keeps asking for his mother."

"When can I go get him? I could leave first thing in the morning."

"Getting him back won't be that simple," Phil explained. "Since he was with his natural father and the laws of two different countries are involved, it's going to take some legal legwork. I'm sure Stuart Leonard will do a good job for you and Jeffey will be home in a few days."

"Thank you. Thank you." Beth shouted as she shook both their hands and then began to dance around the room as they slipped out the door. "Jeffey's coming home. Jeffey's coming home. Thank You, Jesus. Jeffey's coming home."

After several minutes of privately rejoicing, Beth had to share this news with someone. The clock said it was too late to bother Edith. Both she and Roy retired early. She immediately called the crisis line. *This is a crisis,* she told herself. *Jeffey's coming home and I've got to shout it to the world.*

"Hello, crisis center. This is Dan, may I help you?"

"I've already been helped," Beth shouted. "Jeffey's coming home."

seven

A half hour before school started Beth Slater burst into the administration office. "They found Jeffey," she exclaimed excitedly.

"Where was he?" Viola Tomkins asked.

"Mickey had taken him to Calgary and then got himself arrested for possession of cocaine."

"Beth, what are you doing here then?" Grady Walker queried. "You should be on your way to Canada."

"I wish I were," she sighed. "But there's a lot of legal red tape between the two countries. Stuart Leonard is working on it now. Hopefully he'll be home by Thanksgiving."

Teachers and students alike went by the library giving Beth hugs and rejoicing with her. At nine o'clock Beth turned to her supervisor, "Rebecca, would you mind if I take a break and go to the teacher's lounge to use the phone?"

"No problem at all," the librarian assured her. "I can watch the floor while you're gone."

Beth dialed the familiar number and waited for an answer. "Hello, Edith. Guess what happened?"

"They found Jeffey," the older woman replied lightheartedly.

"How'd you know so early? It's scarcely nine o'clock," Beth protested, wanting to be the first one to break the news.

"I see you didn't read the morning paper," Edith chuckled. "It's the headline in the *Herald*."

"I never have time to read the paper until after work," Beth confessed. "There's no need for me to tell anyone else since the entire town knows now."

Edith nodded her head. "I'm sure the coffee shops are buzzing."

"I've got to call my parents now. They had planned to return to Rocky Bluff just as soon as Jeffey was found. I've got to tell them not to come until I have an exact date for his return. I'm going to throw the biggest Thanksgiving bash ever for Jeffey and them."

ॐ

Forty-five minutes before Stuart Leonard's secretary, Pat Crouse, and his paralegal, Libby Reynolds, were due at work, the telephone rang in the Little Big Horn County Attorney's Office. *Who could be calling this time of the morning?* Stuart groaned as he reached for the phone. *I came in early so I wouldn't be disturbed.*

"County Attorney's office. May I help you?"

"Stuart Leonard, please."

"Speaking."

"Mr. Leonard, my name is Greg McIntyre. I'm an attorney in Calgary, Alberta. I've been retained to represent Mickey Kilmer for violating Criminal Code Canada. He's been charged with importing two kilos of cocaine into Canada and illegal possession of a handgun."

"Sounds like Mickey's been a very busy man," Stu broke in. "We're preparing kidnapping charges against him down here for violating the Montana Criminal Code."

"Stu." It was Greg's turn to break in. "We both know you can't make it stick. And even if you could, the Crown will never agree to an extradition hearing on Mickey. Importing drugs into Canada is a major felony up here not to mention illegal possession of a handgun. I sent my paralegal to Helena Tuesday and she obtained a copy of Jeffey's birth certificate from your Bureau of Vital Statistics. It shows Mickey as Jeffey's natural father. In the absence of a court order to the contrary, the natural father has just as much right to custody of the child as the natural mother."

Although Stuart resented the early phone call, he resented foreign interference in the Kilmer case even more. But he understood where Greg was coming from. He even knew what point Greg was going to make next.

"It's going to be next to impossible to make a case of kidnapping against the natural father," Greg chided. "Oh, you might be able to make out a case of custodial interference, but even that's debatable because no court has ever awarded custody of Jeffey to anyone."

"What's your point, Greg?"

"Look, Stu, I'm a good attorney. I can modestly say I'm as good an attorney as you'll find in my country or in yours. But I can't beat this charge against Mickey. Six RCMP Constables were present when Mickey was stopped per your APB and in their search of Mickey's Porsche they found the cocaine and the handgun. It's an open and shut case. Mickey's going to jail all right, but he's going to jail in Alberta, not Montana."

"I can live with that, but we want Jeffey back," Stu stated firmly.

"Here's my point," Greg continued. "We're asking you to drop all charges against Mickey in Montana. In exchange, he will surrender Jeffey without a fight. That way when he gets out of jail up here in three or four years, he won't still have the Montana charge hanging over him."

"I'll have to think on that for a while, Greg, and do a little research to see if I can find a precedent."

"I've already found one for you."

"Your court or mine?"

"Yours," Greg retorted. "Have you read Wilson versus Barlow? It's a recent Montana case."

"No, I haven't," Stu admitted.

"How about reading it and call me back. Call collect if you wish."

"All right, give me a couple of hours, Greg, and I'll get back to you."

"Thanks for your time, Stu, have a nice day."

"You, too. 'Bye for now."

As soon as Stuart hung up the phone he went to his library and read Wilson versus Barlow. In that case, the court held that the statute provides that a person who has left the state does not commit the offense of custodial interference if he returns the individual taken to lawful custody prior to arrest. Greg had done his homework before he called. Stuart was impressed with this brash young Canadian.

Mickey had been arrested, but not by U.S. law officers and he was arrested for possession of cocaine and an illegal handgun, not for kidnapping, not for custodial interference.

Stuart returned to his office and called Milton Eubanks, Chief Judge of the Little Big Horn County District Court. He explained the legal problems he had encountered with the Kilmer case and recommended that they accept Greg's offer.

Judge Eubanks readily agreed. It would not only save

the taxpayers of Little Big Horn County thousands of dollars, but most importantly, the child would be returned to his mother's arms almost immediately.

Stuart dialed Greg's number and was greeted by a pleasant feminine voice with a decidedly French accent. Then Greg came on the line. "Stu, that was fast and you didn't even call collect. What's the verdict, old buddy?"

"We'll go along with you. You set up the time and place for us to pick up Jeffey. I recommend the border crossing station at Sweetgrass."

"No problem. The border crossing station at Sweetgrass it is. How about noon Monday?"

"I'll be there. Say, Greg, when you come can you bring me some Fraser River salmon?"

"I will," chuckled Greg, "if you bring me about four buffalo steaks."

"Consider it a done deal. Oh, by the way, Greg, I don't know whether you're as fine a lawyer as I could find in your country, but you're certainly as fine a lawyer as I could find in mine."

"Thanks for the compliment, Stu." Greg tried to act serious for a moment. "Do you like hockey, Stu?"

"I sure do. I never miss a Bulls home game in Billings and I'll make a bet with you."

"What's your bet?"

"I'll bet you our Canucks can whip your Canucks."

On that frivolous note the two attorneys hung up, looking forward to meeting face-to-face on Monday.

২৯

That Saturday Dan picked up Edith and Roy Dutton, and then Beth Slater for their trip to Running Butte.

"Rebecca Sutherland and I would like to throw a

welcome home party for Jeffey Tuesday afternoon in the library right after school," Edith said as they passed the Rocky Bluff city limits. "We wanted to use the gym but they have basketball practice until seven o'clock."

"Everyone is being so good to me," Beth replied. "I don't know what to say."

"Just to have Jeffey back in Rocky Bluff will be enough," Edith replied. "What arrangements have been made for bringing him home?"

Beth smiled as she thought of being reunited with her giggling child. "Stuart Leonard, Dan, and I are going to drive to Great Falls tomorrow afternoon and get a motel room for the night. It's just too far to make it to Sweetgrass from here by noon."

"I'm along as the chaperon," Dan inserted as he winked at Beth sitting beside him.

"I need all the moral support I can get," Beth responded quickly. "I'm not used to dealing with law enforcement people, attorneys, and customs agents."

"We plan to go back to Great Falls Monday night and leave for home first thing Tuesday morning, so we should be back by two or three o'clock that afternoon," Dan explained.

"That's perfect. You could come directly to the library as soon as you get back in town. Sonya and Patricia said they would bring Jeffey's friends from Kinder University to the party."

"Jeffey will be pleased. He really likes the new friends he's made at the day-care center."

"Rebecca is already collecting gifts for him so he'll have an early Christmas."

"It may be Christmas for him, but Thanksgiving for me,"

Beth responded. "My parents will be coming Tuesday so they should be here in time for the party. It will be the first time they've held their grandson. I've never known them to be this excited before."

"I'm sure there'll be reporters from both the *Herald* and the television station at the celebration. Jeffey has become quite a celebrity throughout the state," Edith reminded her.

"What about all the notices that have gone up all around the country?" Roy queried in his usual practical manner.

"Teresa Lennon has been busy notifying business establishments to take down Jeffey's posters, because the Missing Child has been found. Larry Reynolds immediately put a notification on the On-line Database that Jeffey had been found," Edith answered.

"It looks like you've been a busy bunch," Dan chided. "Nothing can beat the community support of the citizens of Rocky Bluff."

Jean Thompson had the table set with several different salads and sandwiches when the foursome arrived at her new double-wide mobile home. A sweet aroma filled the air. "This looks like quite a feast," Roy exclaimed as she motioned for him to sit at the head of the table.

"It needs to be," she chuckled. "I'm getting free advice. Besides, it gave me a chance to try a recipe that I got from one of my new friends here in Running Butte."

"So what is it I smell?" Edith asked.

Jean's eyes sparkled. "Indian Fry Bread," she replied. "I'm sorry I'll have to ration the portion I give to Roy. It's definitely not designed for a diabetic. Gloria sure loves it."

After they finished lunch, Jean stacked the dishes in the

dishwasher. Then she and Jim led the way across the street to the new store. The exterior of the building was finished, complete with a sign HARKNESS HARDWARE II. Jim put his key into the keyhole, flung the door open, and shouted, "Ta-daah."

The interior walls were framed, but no sheetrock had been hung yet. Sawhorses and lumber cluttered the floor. "If you would all step this way I will show you the front counter over which thousands of dollars of merchandise will pass each month," Jim grinned as he motioned to an empty space close to the door. "In this section will be the household goods and to your right will be yard supplies."

Jim led the gathering through the framework of a partitioned wall. "To your right are the men's and ladies' rest rooms and to your left is the paint room." He observed the investigative looks on Roy and Edith's face and continued, "Of course you will note that the paint room will be well ventilated. We want to be far above code and not even have any cause for suspicion of a fire here."

"Jim, you're doing a great job here," Edith observed. "How soon do you plan to be open?"

"We'd like to be open in February," he replied. "It would mean a lot to the locals not to have to drive into Rocky Bluff for their spring supplies. However, we still have one hitch."

"What's that?" Roy asked.

"I don't have time to learn to run the computer system and Jean is busy getting the medical clinic set up," Jim sighed.

"Another reason, I have trouble understanding computers," Jean explained. "To me it's like, if it doesn't breathe, I can't comprehend it."

Edith hesitated. "This is a long shot, but what are the chances of Larry Reynolds coming to Running Butte to help with the computers? Nancy can handle the Rocky Bluff store."

"Do you think his wife would be willing to leave Stuart Leonard's office?" Beth questioned. "She worked pretty hard to get that paralegal degree. It would be difficult for her to put it behind her now."

"There would have to be a pretty big carrot offered to entice her to come to Running Butte, but anything is possible," Jim exclaimed thoughtfully.

"A very big one," Beth murmured.

"So what do you think of our project so far?" Jim asked as he surveyed the expressions on each of their faces.

"It's almost unbelievable," Edith responded. "George always wanted to build a satellite store, but the timing never seemed right. He would be very proud of what you and Bob have done."

"Now it's my turn," Nancy said as she led the group out the front door of the building. "If you'll follow me just one block south you will find yourself in the waiting room of the Running Butte Medical Center."

Edith took Jim's arm as they slowly walked down the only paved street in Running Butte. "Sorry we can't offer you a sidewalk, but the founding fathers did not foresee any expansion in their community," Jean chuckled.

"You really have to use your imagination on this," Jim teased as he pointed to a vacant lot with string connecting numerous stacks.

"The federal government promised us a building by springtime, but I'm getting a little apprehensive," Jean sighed.

"But if it goes as fast as the store has once they get the frame here it shouldn't be a problem," Jim tried to encourage. "The committee is really working hard to get this up and operational."

"Anyway, the front will be the lobby," Jean explained. "The medical wing will be on the left, complete with a major trauma facility. We hope to be able to fund our own ambulance."

"They think they could save several lives a year if they didn't have to wait for an ambulance to be dispatched from Rocky Bluff," Jim inserted.

Jeans eyes brightened. "The wing on the right will have rooms for miscellaneous services. This is where we'd like to have the crisis center lines installed."

"It would be so much handier to have it adjacent to the medical clinic, than clear across town as it is in Rocky Bluff," Roy noted. "I hope you'll be able to fund it."

"It looks good right now, but we're also trying to get a social worker and a tribal attorney as well."

"That might be your carrot," Beth giggled.

Jean's eyes twinkled. "You mean for Libby?"

"Who knows?" Beth replied.

"The committee has been negotiating with a local man who is at the University of Montana Law School right now," Jim explained. "They're trying to convince him to come home and work as the tribal attorney. Their reservation legal system is in shambles right now and the people are so confused they don't know what to do. They feel like they're neither fish nor fowl."

"We wish you luck," Edith said. "I know these people have been neglected far too long. In fact, Pastor Rhodes has even mentioned the possibility of starting a mission work out here. So many of the people have given up hope and turned to alcoholism."

"Only one or two stay in school until they graduate, so we're fortunate to have one of them finishing law school this spring," Jean said as she looked at her mother. "Mom, you're looking tired. Maybe you'd like to take a short nap before you head back to Rocky Bluff?"

"I guess I am getting a little weary," Edith confessed. "Why don't we head back to your house. I'll take a quick nap while the rest of you plan the new crisis center."

❧

As the sun was setting, Dan stopped his car in front of Beth's apartment. "Thank you for such a lovely day," Beth said as Dan walked her to her door. "It helped make the time go faster until Jeffey is home."

Dan roared. "I hope I mean more to you than just a way to kill time."

"I'm sorry, Dan. I didn't mean it that way. You are a fun person to be around. It's just I don't know how to relax and have fun, especially since Jeffey's been gone."

"Jeffey will be back in your arms Monday and then maybe I can teach you how to trust God, relax, and have fun. I'd like to start tonight but I'm scheduled to work at the crisis center in a half hour."

"I'm looking forward to seeing you tomorrow when we leave for Great Falls," Beth responded. "Just remember you're along only as a chaperon," she chuckled.

eight

"This is your wake-up call," Dan Blair chuckled as Beth answered the phone in room 113 of the Sunrise Inn in Great Falls. "Breakfast is in thirty minutes in the motel restaurant."

"I've been up since five o'clock," Beth replied. "I was too excited to sleep. Just think, in five hours I'll have Jeffey in my arms again."

"Since you're ready, why don't you meet Stu and I in the restaurant in five minutes? Then we can have an early start for Sweetgrass."

"I'll be there." Beth quickly stuffed her curling iron and makeup into her bag, grabbed her coat, and hurried to the restaurant.

"Good morning, Beth," Stuart Leonard greeted as he motioned for her to join them in the booth. "I understand you didn't sleep well last night."

Beth smiled as she slid in beside Dan. "All I could think about was Jeffey. I bet he was totally confused with the entire ordeal."

"All they told me was that he kept saying, 'I want my Mommy'," Stu told her for what seemed the tenth time.

"We called the highway patrol for the road report and they say there's snow on the highway further north so it'd be best if we get an early start," Dan explained as he reached for one of the menus the waitress handed the trio.

The drive to Sweetgrass from Great Falls was uneventful,

and the hours seemed to drag by. Beth felt like a little child every time she asked, "How soon are we going to get there?"

They arrived at the Customs' Office in Sweetgrass at eleven forty-five. The officials on duty had neither seen Attorney Greg McIntyre nor a small child. Beth paced nervously across the lobby, inspecting every car approaching the check station. No one who was traveling with a small child fit the attorney's general description.

"Would you like a cup of coffee while you wait?" the customs agent asked as he sensed her nervousness.

"Yes, that would be nice," she replied as she waited while he filled a styrofoam cup for her. As she was taking her first sip, a brown Bronco stopped in the parking lot. A young man in a business suit got out along with a well-dressed middle-aged woman. The woman opened the door to the back seat and unlatched a child's car seat. She took the child by the hand and walked around the back of the vehicle toward the lobby of the inspection station.

"Jeffey!" Beth shouted as she ran out the door and across the parking lot just as fast as she could.

The child broke away from his caregiver's hand. "Mommy!" he shouted as he ran toward her with his short legs moving just as fast as they could.

Beth picked up her son in the middle of the snow-packed parking lot and held him tight. It was hard to tell which one was crying the hardest. Dan and Stuart stood nearby, with tears in their eyes.

"I take it you're Greg McIntyre," Stu said as he extended his right hand. "I'm Stuart Leonard and this is Dan Blair."

"It's nice meeting both of you," Greg replied as he shook hands with both men and then turned to the woman at his side. "This is Victoria Marshall. She's head of protective services in Calgary. She's been seeing that Jeffey has been getting the best of care."

"It's nice meeting you both," she said as she extended her hand in greeting. "There's no doubt at all who the mother is," she said as she nodded toward the young mother still embracing her child.

The five happy adults went into the lobby to sign the necessary legal papers. While Stuart and Greg shuffled papers, Beth gave Jeffey a new stuffed panda bear that she had purchased at the mall in Great Falls.

"That should about do it," Greg said as he closed his briefcase. "Now, did you bring the buffalo steaks that you promised?" he teased. "I heard they're out of season now."

"Just a moment. I'll have to go to my trunk and get the cooler," Stu replied smugly. "The local grocer keeps a supply in the freezer for the tourists."

Greg's face dropped. "I didn't think you were serious so I didn't bring the Fraser River salmon."

"There's one thing you need to learn," Stu chided. "A Montana attorney always keeps his word."

On the way back to Great Falls Beth and Jeffey sat in the back seat and played nursery rhyme games. Finally, Jeffey fell asleep with a contented smile on his face. Beth memorized every line on his body before she too dozed off. This was the day the entire town of Rocky Bluff had been praying for.

&

"Mrs. Dutton, I hope you don't mind us stopping by unannounced," Suzanne Slater said as Edith opened her door. "Since Beth is on her way to bring Jeffey home we just wanted to come and personally thank you for all you've done for our daughter and grandson."

"Do come in," Edith replied as she motioned for them to enter. "Have you met my husband, Roy Dutton?

"Roy, I'd like you to meet Beth's parents, Suzanne and Ed Slater. I met them briefly at a 'Bring Jeffey Home' Committee meeting."

The couple crossed the room to shake hands with Roy. "We heard so much about you from Beth."

"Please have a seat," Edith urged. "Would you like a cup of coffee?"

"That would be a nice warmer-upper," Ed replied. "It was a long, cold trip from Glasgow, but we wanted to be here when Jeffey and Beth got back."

Edith disappeared to the kitchen and was back within moments with four cups of coffee on a serving tray. "We're planning a 'Welcome Home' party tomorrow at the school library where Beth works and we'd love to have you join us."

"Don't you think our presence would be awkward after we disowned our daughter for so long and did not even acknowledge that we had a grandson?" Suzanne queried.

"We were so angry and foolish when Beth told us she was pregnant," Ed confessed. "We tried to tell her that Mickey was a worthless drifter, but she was sure she could change him."

"When we forbade her from seeing him she started sneaking around to meet him," Suzanne continued. "Her grades started dropping and she seemed totally out of control. I just didn't know what to do."

"I could imagine it was extremely difficult for you," Edith comforted. "Raising teenagers is never easy."

Ed's face lengthened as he stared out the window. "Beth

never actually told us she was pregnant, but when her clothes started getting tight we confronted her. It wasn't a very pretty scene."

"We tried to have her get an abortion so no one would know she'd ever been pregnant but she wouldn't hear of it," Suzanne recalled. "For some strange reason that unborn child was important to her and she refused to consider an abortion. She disappeared the next day. I cried for weeks, and then I turned numb inside. It was like a part of me had died, until I saw Jeffey's picture on the TV news and knew that Beth was all right."

"We're so proud that she stood up to us about an abortion. All we thought about was that she was carrying a product of her sin, not a child as precious as Jeffey," Ed continued.

"Beth told us the last time we were here that Mickey had left Glasgow the day she told him she was pregnant, but had given her three hundred dollars to help pay for her medical bills. She used that money to get a bus ticket to Rocky Bluff." Suzanne took a tissue from her purse and dabbed her eyes. "All she could talk about was all the people here who helped her, especially you and Roy."

"Beth worked very hard to finish her education, obtain a secretarial degree, and get a job," Edith replied. "She's an inspiration to a lot of young girls who have made bad choices in their lives."

"We're just glad you were there through the tough times," Suzanne said. "You did what I should have done. You were a mother to her when she needed it the most. I don't know how I'll ever repay you."

Edith smiled. "You can repay us by starting a brand new relationship with your daughter and grandson. Your attendance at the party tomorrow would mean so much to Beth. It would demonstrate to the community the power of forgiveness on both your parts."

Ed smiled. "Put in those terms, we'll be honored to be there. We brought our video camera and won't miss a precious moment of it."

❧

The next afternoon Stu Leonard pulled into a truck stop on the edge of Rocky Bluff. "I'm sorry to stop so close to home, but I've been driving on empty for the last forty miles and I'm afraid to go a mile further. The service station where I usually fill up on my way home from Great Falls was closed and I've been driving on fumes ever since."

"That's okay," Beth replied. "I need to change Jeffey into some new clothes before his party. I didn't want to dress him at the motel because I was sure he'd have them messed up before we got home."

"You're coming to Jeffey's party at the school library, aren't you, Stu?" Dan asked as Stu inserted the nozzle into the gas tank.

"I'd like to, but I have an appointment with Judge Eubanks at four o'clock. That's one I don't dare be late for."

A half hour later Jeffey walked into the Rocky Bluff High School hand-in-hand with his mother. He felt very important getting to come into the 'big kids' school. However, when Beth opened the door to the library and stepped inside, Jeffey clung tightly to her when a crowd of friends and strangers shouted "Welcome home, Jeffey!" Cameras flashed all around him.

Suddenly Jeffey spotted a group of friends from Kinder University playing in the corner and was immediately in the middle of them, ignoring all the other guests.

"Jeffey, we have some presents we'd like to have you open, " Edith said as she pointed to a table piled high with brightly wrapped gifts.

"You mean these are all for me, Granny Edith?" he grinned.

"They sure are. Maybe your mother could help you open them."

For the next twenty minutes Jeffey opened presents. There was a fire truck from Sonya Turner, a musical toy from Roy and Edith Dutton, and numerous stuffed animals and cars from other community members. Finally, Larry Reynolds brought a large gift from behind the counter.

"I wanted to save the best for last," Larry chuckled. "If Jeffey's going to make a hit in Rocky Bluff High School, there is one thing he's going have to learn young."

Beth's eyes twinkled. "And what's that?"

"Have him open the box and find out," Larry said as he set the box in front of the child.

Jeffey was soon tearing the paper and throwing it in all directions. Beth had to ask for a pair of scissors to help her son open the taped box. Suddenly she started giggling. Inside the box was a nerf ball along with a miniature basketball hoop.

"We have to start teaching them to play basketball young in Rocky Bluff," Larry chided. "We have to keep up our state championship record."

The entire group roared as they remembered Larry's ill-fated basketball days and the community pressures for a winning team.

Beth was extremely conscious of a video camera in the background. Yet, she had little time to respond to its operators. Finally, Jeffey looked up from his toys. "Jeffey, I'd like you to meet your grandma and grandpa," Beth said as she motioned for her parents to come to the front.

Jeffey looked stunned. "I didn't know I had anymore grandmas. I just thought I had Granny Edith."

"This is my mother and father, your grandma and grandpa," she explained as she embraced them both. Not wanting to be left out on any loving, without a moment hesitation Jeffey ran immediately into his Grandma Slater's arms for a hug. Not a single eye in the room was dry. This was the miracle the Slaters had almost missed because of their lack of forgiveness.

❧

Jim Thompson and Bob Harkness poured over catalogs and inventory sheets far into the night while their wives spent a leisurely evening with Roy and Edith Dutton. A December snow was slowly inundating the entire state.

"I'm glad we brought a change of clothes so we can spend the night," Jim remarked as the two walked to Bob's hardware store. "I've already slid into the ditch once this season. We were fortunate that time, but I don't want to push my luck again."

"At least we won't be able to complain about not having a white Christmas this year," Bob noted.

"That is unless a Chinook wind comes in at the last minute," Jim reminded him. "A couple of Christmases ago, when we came for the holidays, there was fourteen inches of snow on the ground when we went to bed and it was all gone the next morning."

"Now back to the books," Bob sighed as the two gathered around the computer screen. "It looks like our best move would be to keep the inventory level at the Running

Butte store at one half of the level here for at least the first year."

"I guess if I needed something in a hurry I could send someone to Rocky Bluff to get it," Jim responded as he refilled his coffee cup. "I like the idea of having internal modems and faxes to link our two systems, but I'm still concerned about doing the book work and managing the store at the same time. Computers have never been my forte. I wish there was some way I could steal Larry Reynolds from you."

Bob thought for a moment, "That would be an ideal situation, but Libby is pretty entrenched in the county attorney's office."

"We've done some pre-work and we might have a paralegal job for her in Running Bluff."

Bob surveyed his brother-in-law with amazement. "Come on," he chucked. "The only thing Running Bluff has going for it is the soon-to-be-opened Harkness Hardware II."

"You sure underestimate the influence of your sister," Jim chided. "She's nearly singledhandedly taken on the Bureau of Indian Affairs. Besides helping get the medical clinic open she is trying to get an ambulance service, a home health care worker, a social worker, a crisis center, and a Tribal Attorney for the reservation people."

"I see I should make it to Running Butte more often just to keep up on things," Bob replied as he visualized his vivacious sister. "Now that Jay's old enough to drive, I've been sending him with the needed supplies."

"They broke ground for the medical clinic last week and Jean made sure there was a wing for social services." Jim nearly exploded with pride. "Last week Jean drove to Missoula with the Chief of the Tribal Council to try to convince Stephen Yellowtail to come back to the reservation after he graduates from law school in June."

"Were they successful?"

"I think so, but they have no final agreement yet," Jim explained. "He's pretty aggressive and is requesting suitable housing along with office space and clerical and paralegal help before he agrees to come. The last tribal council meeting voted to meet his demands."

"I know where they can get an excellent paralegal, don't you?" Bob winked.

"Why don't we present this proposition to Larry first thing in the morning and give him and Libby time to think about it?" Jim suggested. "The paralegal position would have to be advertised to the public and meet all government regulations, but with Libby's training and experience she would be a shoo-in for the position."

ॐ

Larry Reynolds stomped the snow off his cowboy boots as he entered the backdoor of Harkness Hardware Store the next morning. "Kind of cold out there," he shuddered as he rubbed his hands together and took off his parka.

"Hi, Larry," Bob shouted out to him. "When you get your coat off, join Jim and me in the office. We have something we want to discuss with you."

"I hope it's good," Larry responded as he entered the office. "I need something to warm me up this morning."

Bob filled Larry's mug. "How would a cup of coffee do for a starter?"

Larry surveyed the pair with suspicion. They had something up their sleeve. "Yeah, sure," he replied.

"Larry, you look like you don't trust us," Jim teased. "Why, we're about to offer you the opportunity of your lifetime."

Larry raised his eyebrows. "Now that sounds like an offer I can't refuse."

"You've learned our computer system backwards and forwards since we put it in," Bob began, trying to chose his words carefully. "Since we're expanding we really need your services in Running Butte. Would you and Libby consider a transfer there?"

"Where would I live? The few livable houses there are all owned by long-term residents," Larry protested.

"There's land on the edge of town where you could put a mobile home," Jim responded. "We could help you get a good deal on a brand new one."

"I know Libby would hate to leave her job with Stuart Leonard," Bob inserted. "But there's a good possibility of a paralegal job with the Tribal Attorney's Office that's opening soon."

"It might not be as difficult as you think to get her to quit her job," Larry replied with a smile.

Both men exchanged puzzled glances. The paralegal job for the Little Big Horn County Attorney was a coveted position.

"Libby hasn't told anyone yet, but she just found out she's pregnant and she's concerned that taking care of two children and working in such a high pressure job might be too much for her. I think she might be amenable to a low-profile job for a while. We'll talk about it and I'll let you know in a few days."

"Sounds like a fair deal," Jim replied. "If Libby has any questions about the job with the Tribal Attorney she might give Jean a call. It's exciting being on the ground floor of several projects at the same time."

nine

"Beth, remember when Jeffey was missing you told me you didn't know how to relax and have fun?" Dan queried as they sat in her living room watching TV together after Jeffey had gone to bed.

Beth flushed. "Yes. I was really uptight then. I just didn't know what to do with myself without Jeffey. He'd become my entire life."

"Now that Jeffey's home and the holiday season is over, I think it's time you learn to have some fun in your life."

"Working full time and then coming home and taking care of Jeffey and the apartment, there's not much time for anything else."

"When you're busy helping everyone else, that's the time when you need a special time for yourself, otherwise you burn out and don't enjoy anything," Dan insisted.

"You're probably right." Beth sighed and then she giggled. "The high school kids can often get as demanding as my four-year-old son."

"Then let's see what we can do to help you learn to have fun," Dan said as he took her hand. "What do you like to do?"

"All I've ever done in my spare time is watch TV. I know that makes me sound like a boring couch potato, but since Jeffey was born I haven't had the money or the time to do anything else."

"What did you like to do when you were still in school?"

"Not much," Beth confessed. "I was too shy to make

95

many friends. I would occasionally go to a basketball game with one of my girlfriends, but when Mickey and I started dating all we did was cruise around town. I didn't do anything with my girlfriends after that."

"Did you participate in any sports?"

"Nope. I was afraid everyone would laugh at me. I guess I was a pretty self-conscious kid."

"Most young teens miss out on a lot of positive experiences because of a low self-esteem, but now that you're older you've learned that the only ones you need to satisfy is God and yourself," Dan reminded her. "You can forget about what other people think."

"I used to spend a lot of time worrying about what other people thought about me, but now I've noticed that people are so busy worrying about their own problems that they don't have time to think about me," Beth chuckled.

"Is there a certain sport you'd like to learn, but are afraid to try?" Dan queried.

Beth thought a moment. "I always thought tennis looked like fun, but we don't have any indoor courts in Rocky Bluff. The regular tennis courts at the country club don't open until spring."

"In Montana our winter sports are pretty much limited to skiing and snowmobiling," Dan noted as he visualized Big Sky Ski Lodge outside of Bozeman where he used to ski as a teenager.

"Even if I'm a native from the coldest part of the state, I still can't stand the cold," Beth snickered.

Dan shook his head in amusement. "If you don't like the cold, that eliminates almost everything." He paused for a moment before continuing. "What about bowling? The Westend Bowling Alley has quite a few leagues."

The thought of meeting different people and just relaxing intrigued Beth, but a practical cloud enveloped her.

"No one would want someone as inexperienced as I am on their team."

"I'm pretty rusty myself, but maybe if we practice a lot this year, by fall we'd be ready for regular leagues." Dan chuckled. "If we weren't, no one would be the wiser and we wouldn't embarrass ourselves by pulling down the team scores."

"I thought you weren't interested in what other people thought of you," Beth teased.

Dan grinned sheepishly. "Just part of my male ego." He hesitated as he gazed into her deep blue eyes. "How about asking one of your high school students if they could come and baby-sit Jeffey Friday night while we go bowling?"

"I've never used a teenage sitter before," Beth cautioned. "They get kind of expensive."

"Don't worry about a thing," Dan assured her. "I'll pay her and give her a ride. Do you know anyone who might be interested in earning two or three dollars for sitting here watching your TV while Jeffey sleeps?"

Beth thought a moment and then her eyes brightened. "I have one student assistant who might be interested. I could ask her tomorrow."

"Great," Dan replied as he squeezed her hand. "Be sure and find out where she lives so I can pick her up."

ße

Friday night Beth and Dan had more laughs and enjoyed themselves more at the Westend Bowling Alley than Beth had ever thought possible. For the first time in her life she felt she was truly a woman with her own identity, not just Jeffey's Mommy, or even worse, a single mother. She learned about strikes and spares, and most importantly, how to avoid gutter balls.

After a couple hours of bowling, Dan suggested, "Let's

go to the Pizza Palace to top off the evening. I'm just not ready for this evening to end."

Beth smiled. "Sounds great," she replied. A mischievous twinkle came into her eyes. "See, I didn't have any trouble at all learning how to relax and have fun."

"Well, I don't know about that," Dan said as he helped her with her coat. "I think you'll need another lesson next Friday night. Having fun could be a pretty difficult skill to learn."

"That'd be marvelous," Beth responded. "If I can't get one of the high school girls to baby-sit, maybe Liz who lives across the hall wouldn't mind watching my TV instead of her own."

A few minutes after midnight when Beth closed the door behind Dan and the baby-sitter whom he was driving home, a warmth enveloped her. *I've never had this much fun before in my life,* she mused. *Dan was always with me for support during those awful days without Jeffey, but I thought I was just a charity case he was helping. Tonight was different. I've never felt this way before. We didn't talk about my problems, we just relaxed and had fun.*

The mood of the previous evening remained with Beth the next day and she was anxious to share it with one of her best friends. After lunch she bundled Jeffey in his new snowsuit and drove to Edith Dutton's home.

"You look cheerful and all aglow," Edith said as she greeted Beth with a quick hug.

"I didn't realize it showed that much," Beth giggled as she took off her coat. "I guess it's safe to say that I had more fun last night than I ever thought possible."

"So what happened? I'm dying to hear what has brought our sweet, serious Beth out of her shell."

"That's just what Dan called me. . . serious," Beth replied as the pair made themselves comfortable at the kitchen table and Jeffey opened up his toy bag on the floor nearby.

Edith nodded with understanding. "You've had to grow up in a hurry and have missed many activities that others your age have enjoyed."

"Dan's trying to bring that to a screeching halt."

Edith's eyes brightened. "I take it your relationship is becoming more than a benevolent concern of his," she teased.

"We did have a lot of fun together last night," Beth admitted, "and we're planning to go out again next Friday."

"Good for you. I'm glad you're beginning to realize that although you have the responsibility of a beautiful child, you can still have a life of your own."

Beth stared into space for a few moments before she spoke. "I've never felt this way about anyone before," she whispered. "Not even when I thought I was madly in love with Mickey."

"Mature love is different from teenage love," Edith reminded her. "It can see you through both the good times and the bad. It doesn't have the roller coaster effect that you see in today's high school students."

Beth again was slow to respond. "I never really thought of this as love. It's just I'm comfortable with Dan. We can laugh together, cry together, or just sit in silence and it doesn't make any difference."

"That's how you know when you've found Mr. Right," Edith replied. "When they feel as comfortable as an old shoe. Men of excitement and glamour may come and go, but life is not excitement and glamour. It's day-to-day events, highlighted with special milestones."

"But I can't fall in love," Beth sighed. "Not now. Not after what has happened."

Edith was puzzled as she surveyed the young woman

across from her. "What terrible thing has happened that would keep you from being loved and loving in return?"

Tears filled Beth's eyes. "I had a child out of wedlock. After Jeffey's disappearance was covered nationwide, the entire world knows about my sin."

"But God forgave you a long time ago," Edith reminded Beth as she patted her hand. "And now even your parents have forgiven you. Why don't you forgive yourself?"

"Sometimes I think I have and then other times I still feel so guilty."

"Beth, it's time to let go of the past and go on with your life. You have a good education, a good job, and a beautiful child. Don't let the mistakes of your youth damage the rest of your life," Edith pleaded. "You're an entirely different person now."

"Sometimes when I'm alone and depressed these things keep coming back to haunt me." Beth shrugged her shoulders. "It's like a thief trying to sneak in and steal my happiness."

How often Edith had faced similar situations herself, but through the years she had developed a strong mental discipline. "Don't let the black thoughts destroy you. Every time one crosses your mind remind yourself that Jesus is stronger than your memories and He'll protect you from your own destructive thoughts."

Beth's eyes brightened as the tears disappeared. "I'll try to oust the annoying memories when they occur," she responded. "But it's going to take a lot of practice."

"You've conquered a lot of problems in your short life," Edith reminded her. "I'm sure you can get control of this one as well. Just don't let your memories stand in the way of developing a relationship with Dan, or anyone else."

Beth beamed. The weight of her past felt like it was lifted from her shoulders. She could begin to admit the possibility that she might be falling in love. . . real love, for the first time in her life.

❧

Larry Reynolds waited until Saturday night after Vanessa was in bed before he brought up Jim Thompson's offer. "Libby," he began as he laid the newspaper beside him on the sofa. "Have you done any more thinking about what you'd like to do after the other baby comes?"

"I really don't know what to do," Libby sighed. "That's why I haven't told anyone I'm pregnant. That's the first thing they'll ask me. 'How much time are you going to take off work? Are you going to be able to work and care for two children?'"

"I'm going to leave that decision up to you," Larry responded gently. "I know it will be a lot of work to do both. It would be tight but if we budget carefully we might be able to get along on just my salary."

"I know," Libby sighed, "but I've worked so hard to get my paralegal education and if I don't keep up to date I'll have trouble getting back in the job market when the kids get older."

"I had an interesting offer that might make a difference." Larry hesitated. "I've been waiting until we had some time alone to discuss it."

"So, what's the other possibility?" Libby queried. "I feel pretty indecisive at this point."

"Bob called me into his office when Jim Thompson was in town last week and asked me if I wanted to work at the Running Butte store," Larry explained as he studied his wife's face for a reaction. "They think I've learned their computer system so well I'd be a lot of help there. Since I've worked so closely with Nancy here they think they'd maintain a much more consistent bookkeeping system if I used the same procedures in that store."

"What did you tell them?"

"I told them I'd think about it and talk it over with you. They both realize how important your job is for you right now, but they didn't know you were pregnant."

"I bet as a proud father you broke the news," Libby chided.

"Well, I was forced to when they had a possibility of a paralegal job for you in Running Butte, but I told them not to tell their wives or Edith until you could break the news."

Libby and Larry discussed the future baby along with the pros and cons of moving to Running Butte far into the night. When they crawled into bed that night they had both agreed it was a good opportunity for the entire family.

The next afternoon while Larry and Vanessa were taking their Sunday afternoon nap, Libby drove to the Dutton residence.

"Libby, it's so good to see you," Edith greeted as she invited the young woman into her living room. "Since you've been working we haven't had much time to spend together."

"I know," Libby agreed meekly. "It's been much too long."

Edith and Roy and Libby visited about routine life in Rocky Bluff before Libby explained the real reason of her visit. "Larry and I have some good news that we've been keeping to ourselves for sometime."

"Let me guess," Edith said with a gleam in her eyes. "You're expecting another little one."

"Did Larry tell you?" Libby scowled good-naturedly.

Edith giggled. "You have that motherly glow about you. You're just radiant."

"It can't be that obvious," Libby protested. "I'm sure someone told you."

"That will always be my secret," Edith replied. "When

is the baby due?"

"The middle of June, hopefully on my birthday."

"Do you plan to take a leave of absence from work?" Roy queried. "I know Stuart Leonard would be lost without you."

"Larry and I are talking about it, but we haven't completely decided," Libby explained. "Did you know Bob and Jim offered Larry a job at Running Butte?"

"Yes, we discussed it while we were there several weeks ago, but we didn't know if it was possible or not," Edith replied. "Everyone knew how well you liked your job."

"I do like it, but with a second child to take care of I don't think I'll be able to do it justice," Libby explained. "So moving to Running Butte isn't out of the question. What do you think?"

"Of course, it's something you and Larry will have to decide," Edith replied, "but perhaps a change of scenery would be good for you."

"I've often thought about that," Libby replied. "We have so many memories here. Not all of them are good. I keep wondering if people are still influenced by Larry's past whenever they see us."

"Larry has been a wonderful testimony to the community that people can change," Roy responded, "but some people refuse to let people change. I think it helps make them feel bigger when in actuality it only shows how small they are."

"Not only what people think about us bothers us, but even more importantly, I still have memories that are triggered every time I drive past the house we used to have on Frontage Road. Every time I pass the high school I think about the worst day in Larry's life," Beth replied as she gazed aimlessly out the window.

"Then maybe moving is the best thing for you," Edith

responded. "I've never believed that a person should run from their problems, but both of you have overcome a lot of obstacles. If you moved, you would leave Rocky Bluff victoriously."

Libby smiled. "That's what I've been thinking. I think I'd like a fresh beginning and no time is better than when we have another child on the way."

Just then the Dutton's doorbell rang. When Roy opened the door, there stood Larry holding Vanessa. "Larry, do come in. We were just talking about you."

"I'm sure you were," he laughed. He gave his wife a quick kiss as Vanessa reached for her mother. "Vanessa and I woke up and decided we hadn't visited the Dutton's in a long while.

"I suppose Libby has told you the good news," Larry grinned.

"Of course," Roy answered. "I just don't know how you kept it quiet for as long as you did."

"We just wanted to know what to do before we started broadcasting the news, but word has a way of getting around Rocky Bluff ahead of us."

"That's life in a little town," Edith replied.

"We'll have to get used to it," Larry replied. "If Libby is agreeable it looks like we'll be living in an even smaller town."

"I was leaning that way before," Libby said as she took her husband's hand, "but after talking with Roy and Edith I'm sure that's what I want to do."

"Not everyone gets a second chance in life the way we have," Larry replied. "This could be one of the best things that ever happened to us." Larry put his arm around Edith and gave her a warm hug. "It seems that my worst enemy has become my best friend."

ten

The sharp ring aroused Dan Blair. He reached sleepily for the phone. "Hello."

"Hello, Dan, this is Jean Thompson." She hesitated as she noted the slowness in his voice. "Did I awaken you?"

Dan rolled over and studied the red numbers on his alarm clock. Ten thirty-five. "I should have been up a long time ago," he admitted. "I worked late at the center last night so I slept in a little. Thanks for calling, I was planning on getting some book work done before noon. What can I do for you?"

"Jim and I will be coming to Rocky Bluff this afternoon and I was wondering if we could get together and discuss the new crisis center for Running Butte."

"I'd love to. Where would you like to meet?"

"How about at mother's at two o'clock? That way they can have some input as well."

Dan was now fully awake. "Sounds good. I'll see you at Edith's at two."

Jean hung up the phone and stood in her kitchen window, marveling at the construction on the new medical center going on just a couple blocks down the street. *A month ago it looked like it would be a couple years before they would begin work on the building and now the exterior is nearly completed. At this rate it's going to be open about the same time as the hardware store.*

That afternoon Jean, Edith, Roy, and Dan each enjoyed

a cup of coffee and carrot cake in the Dutton's living room. Jean had a yellow tablet paper and pen beside her. "Dan, what is the first step I need to take in organizing a crisis center?"

Dan looked at her across the room. "Roy, I think you'd be a better one to answer her questions. What were some of the first things you did in starting the one here in Rocky Bluff?"

Roy set his coffee cup on the end table beside him. "First, and most important, you'll need volunteers. That's where good advertising comes in."

"When I first volunteered, it was in answer to an ad in the *Herald*," Edith recalled. "However, without a community newspaper you'll have a bigger challenge on your hands."

"Whenever anything is going on in Running Butte a sign is always posted in the local grocery store," Jean grinned. "Everyone in town gets to the store at least once a week. Also, Pastor Rhodes is very good about putting community announcements in the church bulletin."

"I'm glad our church established a mission to the Native Americans at Running Butte," Edith noted. "I know our congregation worked extremely hard renovating an old abandoned school there into a church. It's quite a sacrifice for Pastor Rhodes to drive out there every Sunday afternoon, but he says he loves the people there."

"Those who attend his services really appreciate all that he's doing and each week we gain a few more worshippers," Jean replied.

The foursome remained quiet as each entertained his or her own thoughts of the enormity of the challenges in Running Butte. Finally Roy broke the silence. "Jean, I hope you get this crisis center off the ground as soon as possible," he said. "I heard that the suicide rate among those on the reservation is almost three times the rate for all other races in our country. Do you have a place and time to meet in mind?"

"I arranged to use the church fellowship hall every Saturday afternoon at three o'clock," Jean explained. "I would like to have some of your specialists from Rocky Bluff come up and talk to us. They could stay overnight with Jim and I and attend church with us the following day."

"That sounds like an excellent plan," Edith encouraged. "You've put a lot of thought into this project."

Jean then turned to Dan who was lost in thought. "Dan, do you think you could prepare a training program for me and arrange for guest speakers when necessary?"

"I thought you'd never ask," he grinned. "I could bring the speakers with me when I come. Probably the same ones who share with our volunteers wouldn't mind taking a Saturday afternoon drive with me. Also, there's a certain young lady I know, who has a great deal of personal interest in the success of crisis centers, who would like to accompany me."

The three exchanged knowing glances. "Looks like things are getting pretty serious between you and Beth," Roy chided.

Dan's face became somber. "I wish they were more serious than they are," he replied. "I think because she has been hurt so badly in her life that she's afraid to love anyone for fear she will be hurt again."

Edith surveyed the handsome young man beside her. "Dan, you've been just the thing she needs," she assured him. "Little by little she'll relax and come around. Just give her a little more time."

"I know," Dan sighed. "Maybe I'm just more ready for a permanent relationship than she is. Perhaps the age difference is a problem."

"At your age, eight years doesn't seem like a lot," Edith replied. "Beth has had to accept more responsibilities than most twenty-year-olds. She needs time to learn to trust her own feelings. Life has changed so fast for her these last few months."

"We're all proud of her," Roy added. "She's going to make someone a mighty fine wife some day."

Dan grinned at the others and then the conversation went back to who should be invited to speak to the Running Butte volunteers. They were motivated by the memory of the crisis center's success with Beth. By the time her husband came to pick her up, Jean had five pages of notes.

Now that the planning of the Running Butte Crisis Center was in the competent hands of Dan Blair, Jean Thompson was able to turn her undivided attention to obtaining a tribal attorney for the members of the reservation. The next week she and Chief Joseph Black Hawk drove to the campus of the University of Montana in Missoula where they met with Stephen Yellowtail.

"Steve, we've made the most generous offer we possibly can, to convince you to come back to Running Butte as our tribal attorney," Chief Black Hawk began as the trio met in the lobby of the law school. "We must have a final commitment now, otherwise we will have to begin looking elsewhere. We have to act when the funding is available."

"Well, I have been offered a prestigious position with a law firm in Washington D.C., but I had the feeling they were only trying to meet some kind of quota. They didn't seem at all interested in my ability as a lawyer," the law student sighed. "Besides, I would never be happy in a big city."

"There's something about the wide open spaces and the call of the land that's inbred in us," Chief Black Hawk replied. "It's just part of being an Indian. Something we can all be proud of."

A look of determination spread across Steve's face. "I can't leave Montana while my own people suffer injustices and I have the skill and training to help them. I plan to move back to the reservation as soon as I graduate in June."

Chief Black Hawk could not conceal his delight. "Great," he exclaimed. "We'll try to have everything ready for your arrival. That's Jean's job."

"Steve, if you have any questions or problems in the transition feel free to contact me," Jean said, knowing the reluctance of many Native Americans to ask for help.

Steve lowered his eyes. "Yes. . . sure."

"I brought along the floor plans of several mobile homes which we could have situated on a lot within three blocks of where your office will be," Jean explained as she took a manila file folder from her briefcase. "All of these come completely furnished—however, you may choose to substitute your own furniture if you'd like."

"My tastes are rather basic, so whatever interior design you choose will be fine with me," Steve replied as he thumbed through the pictures and brochures from the mobile home dealer in Rocky Bluff. "However, I do have one request. I would like a three-bedroom. I need an extra bedroom for when my family comes to visit and one for a home office. I'm a big one in getting up on the middle of the night to work."

Jean opened a colorful brochure and placed it before the young law student. "How does this one look?"

Steve studied the floor plan and description for a few minutes in silence before he spoke. "I like it," he replied seriously. "I've never lived in anything that nice before."

"Good," Jean smiled. "I'll have the dealer order it and he'll have it ready for you by the middle of June."

Chief Black Hawk leaned back in his chair. "Another hurdle you'll need to cross is passing both the Tribal and the Montana State Bar Exams," he began. "We've arranged for the County Attorney of Little Big Horn County to help you study for the state bar exam. Stuart Leonard has a brilliant mind and I'm sure he'll be a big help."

"Also, Stuart's paralegal will be moving to Running Butte before the new hardware store opens," Jean inserted. "Her name is Libby Reynolds and she comes highly recommended. Of course, you can hire your own staff, but she's more than qualified for the position."

Steve's eyes filled with tears. "I'm so glad someone is finally helping my people. It breaks my heart every time I go home and see the misery on the reservation."

"It's interesting," Chief Black Hawk explained. "Once a local church in Rocky Bluff became interested in our people and our problems, things began to happen. They were even able to shake up the government bureaucracy to get the promised government programs started."

"Do you have a doctor, yet?" Steve queried. "It would be a shame to have a fancy building and no doctor."

"Right now we have a physician's assistant lined up to come," Jean explained. "He's a member of the Blackfoot Tribe in Browning. He'll be coming in June when he finishes his training. The hospital and doctors in Rocky Bluff have promised to work closely with our clinic."

Chief Black Hawk looked proudly at the woman beside him. "Jean was Director of Nursing at the Chamberlain, Idaho, hospital before moving to Running Butte and she'll be in charge of the nurses and nurses' aides in the clinic. We're getting a lot more experience than we'd ever dreamed possible."

"I'm glad to hear that," Steve replied. "I just read some alarming statistics about reservation health care that made me want to leave law school and go to medical school. However, my queasiness at the sight of blood was the deciding factor to stay where I am."

"The statistics are frightening," Chief Black Hawk admitted. "Especially when those statistics are your own family and friends. Three times more Indian babies die of Sudden Infant Death Syndrome than any others. The pregnancy rate among high school-aged Indian women in Montana is more than three times greater than the rate for all other women ages fifteen to nineteen. Diabetes and cirrhosis of the liver are also rampant on the reservation."

Steve shook his head sadly. "I can hardly wait to get back home to help my people. If there's someone coming to care for their medical needs, I'll do my best to meet their legal needs."

❧

That winter, basketball fever had again swept Rocky Bluff. This year not even Dan Blair could avoid the enthusiasm. Wednesday night he gave Beth a call. "Beth, I know we were planning to go bowling Friday night, but how would you like to go to the high school basketball game with me instead?"

"That sounds like fun," she promptly replied. "Since I've been working in the library I'm getting to know some of the players. I rarely went to the ball games when I was in high school, but now basketball has an entirely different appeal to me."

"Then you have a lot of making up to do," Dan chuckled. He hesitated before continuing, "Do you think Jeffey would like to come with us?"

"He'd love it. Larry Reynolds gave him a toy basketball set at his welcome home party and he plays with it all the time."

"The game is supposed to be a real barn burner," Dan continued. "They're playing Lewistown for the championship. The winner will advance to the Class A Tournament in Billings."

"I overheard the kids talking about the game in the library today. They're all excited about it. I hear the combination of Ryan Reynolds and Jay Harkness is unstoppable."

"We'll see if they're that good," Dan chuckled. "I'll pick you and Jeffey up about seven o'clock."

"I'll be looking forward to it. See you Friday night."

Jeffey could scarcely contain himself at the thought of going to a real basketball game. When they arrived at the Rocky Bluff High School gym that Friday night, he insisted on a bag of popcorn and a small cup of pop before he even entered the gym.

Dan selected seats midway up the bleachers near the half-way line of the court. The teams were still doing their warm-up drills as the threesome made themselves comfortable. Jeffey was mesmerized with the pep band as they played all of the upbeat favorites. He was soon clapping his hands in time with the music along with the cheerleaders. Suddenly everyone rose to their feet and sang the school song while the cheerleaders did their acrobatic stunts.

"Wow, those girls are good," Dan whispered. "Cheerleaders never did those kind of feats when I was in high school."

"They spend a lot of time in the weight room building up their strength so they can lift each other that way. The cheerleaders are even stronger than some of the guys, much to their frustration," Beth snickered.

Suddenly a hush fell across the crowd as they began to introduce the team members. "Number twenty-three, Ryan Reynolds," the speaker shouted. The Rocky Bluff supporters cheered. "Number fourteen, Jay Harkness." The crowd cheered even louder. The noise level increased as the other members of the team were introduced. Finally, the crowd was seated, the referee blew his whistle, and the game began.

The score remained close throughout the first three quarters. First Rocky Bluff would lead by two or three points and then Lewistown would lead. For a while it looked like the high school students were right. . . Ryan and Jay were unstoppable.

Jeffey could scarcely contain his excitement as he sat between Beth and Dan. Dan had almost as much fun watching Jeffey enjoy the game as he did watching the game himself. During a time-out, Jeffey looked up at Dan, "Gee, you're a lot of fun," he giggled. "You're almost like having a real daddy."

Beth and Dan exchanged nervous glances. "You're a lot of fun yourself," Dan said as he tousled the boy's hair. "I'd like to consider you as my son."

Jeffey suddenly became serious. "I had a daddy for three days once but he was mean and went to jail. You're a lot nicer than he was."

Beth bit her lip to keep back her tears while Dan reached behind the child's back and gave her hand a comforting squeeze. "I hope the three of us will get to do a lot of things together," he replied just as the buzzer rang, announcing the end of the time-out.

As the minutes ticked away on the clock, the game became even more intense. Both teams resorted to a run-and-gun style of play. Suddenly, the referee blew his whistle and pointed to Jay as he held up one finger on his left hand and four fingers on his right. Jay walked meekly to the bench.

"What happened to Jay?" Jeffey queried.

"He had too many fouls and the rules say if you've touched another player too many times you're out of the game," Dan explained.

A Lewistown player advanced to the free throw line. He shot and made it. His next shot swished the net without even hitting the backboard. Lewistown was now three points ahead with only twenty seconds left in the game.

Rocky Bluff worked the ball down the floor, but Lewistown increased their defensive pressure. With eight seconds left Ryan Reynolds shot and made it. The score was now Rocky Bluff seventy-seven and Lewistown seventy-eight. Lewistown took the ball and slowed the game to nearly a standstill.

"Why don't they run and shoot like they've been doing?" Jeffey asked.

"They don't want to run the risk of Rocky Bluff getting possession of the ball and making another basket," Dan explained.

Suddenly the buzzer sounded. The game was over. A heavy gloom settled over the Rocky Bluff supporters as they began filing out of the gymnasium.

"It's too bad they lost," Beth said as they began putting on their coats. "This game meant so much to the entire school. They haven't had a championship team since Larry Reynolds led the team six years ago."

"The kids may think so, but life isn't over," Dan chuckled through his own disappointment. "Jay and Ryan are only juniors. They're sure to take the team to the Class A State Championship next year."

"Dan, I wish I had your spirit of optimism in spite of disappointment," Beth sighed as she looked into his steel blue eyes. "You're the best encourager I've ever known."

Dan wrapped his right arm around Beth while he took Jeffey's chubby hand in his left. "The two of you mean more to me than I can ever express in a crowded gym," he laughed.

eleven

"Jeffey finally fell asleep," Beth sighed as she sank into the cushions of her sofa. "The flu that's going around this winter is really wretched."

Dan put his arm around the tired young mother. "It's tough to see these little guys be so miserable and not be able to do much to help them."

"I'm glad you were able to come and stay with him while I was at work," Beth responded. "That's one of the disadvantages of being a working mother. . . what to do when the kids are sick and can't go to day care."

"Since I've been taking the night shift at the crisis center, this worked out perfect for both of us. I love that child as if he were my own."

Beth smiled as she stretched her feet upon the footstool and rested her head upon Dan's chest. "He thinks the world of you. That seems to be all he can talk about lately. . . When's Dan coming?"

Dan paused a moment and admired the young woman beside him. "I'd like to make our relationship more permanent. Dropping in every few days, going out to eat or going bowling or to a ball game seems pretty limiting. Beth, will you marry me so we could spend the rest of our lives together?"

Beth sat in stunned silence. Tears filled her eyes. "Dan, you deserve someone better than I. You deserve someone who's not tainted by a sinful past that keeps coming back to haunt her."

"Beth, don't be ridiculous. We've been through this many times before. You're not tainted. While you were a silly teenager you fell in love with a number one jerk. God has forgiven you for what has happened and has blessed you with a beautiful son. Please try to forgive yourself."

"I'm trying," Beth confessed, "but it's so difficult at times. I don't understand how you could love me like you do."

"I love you because you're a mature, compassionate young woman whom I enjoy spending my time with." Dan's voice became emphatic. "We've grown closer together through the good times and the bad. There seems to be nothing we haven't shared."

"Doesn't being eight years older than me bother you?" Beth queried.

"If you were fourteen and I was twenty-two it would make a big difference, but you are a mature woman now. After you get out of your teens, age becomes irrelevant. Please put aside your fears and say yes."

Beth again sat in silence. "I want to say yes," she stammered, "but I need more time to think about it. I made such a big mistake five years ago that I don't trust my own decisions."

Dan pulled Beth tighter against himself. "I'll give you all the time you need. I know this is the biggest decision you'll ever make in your life."

Suddenly Dan's eyes rested at the clock over the television. "Beth, I didn't realize it was getting so late. I'm supposed to be at the crisis center at nine o'clock. It could be a busy evening."

The couple embraced quickly and rose to their feet. "I'll

call you tomorrow," Dan promised. "I'm afraid I'll have to spend most of Saturday at the center, but I'll be by first thing Sunday to take you and Jeffey to church, providing he's feeling better."

Beth smiled as Dan slipped out the door. "Thanks for all you've done. I don't know what I'd do without you."

As Beth laid restlessly in her bed that night the words *I don't know what I'd do without him* kept running through her mind. She pictured herself alone with Jeffey in five years. She would do her best to raise him properly, but it would be hard to face life's challenges alone.

She then pictured Dan across the kitchen table every night discussing the days happenings. She pictured him coaching Jeffey's little league team as she sat proudly in the stands. She imagined family camping trips into the nearby mountains. *Dear God,* she prayed. *I want a normal married life so badly. Do I really deserve it after what I've done?*

Suddenly a peace came over Beth. *Christ died so that I could have life and have it abundantly. Why shouldn't Jeffey and I be happy and have a normal family life? We both love Dan and he loves us. I want to talk this over with Edith before I give Dan a firm commitment. I don't want to hurt him in the slightest way.*

❧

"That show wasn't worth watching," Edith sighed. "I wish I'd spent the evening with a good book. I think I'll head off to bed now. Are you coming, Roy?"

Edith looked over at her husband. His eyes were glazed. Without saying a word, he stood and then crumpled to the floor. Edith was immediately at his side. "Roy, are you all right?" she pleaded as she reached for his pulse.

The elderly gentleman did not respond except for several involuntary muscle spasms. Edith ran to the phone and dialed 9-1-1.

"Rocky Bluff Emergency Response. May I help you?"

"Yes," Edith responded breathlessly. "I need an ambulance at the Roy Dutton residence at nine twenty-three Maple Street right away. Roy has collapsed and won't respond to anything."

"We'll have an ambulance right there, Mrs. Dutton," the dispatcher responded. "Please try to remain calm until they arrive and turn on an outside light on so they can read the house numbers."

Edith returned to the living room and knelt by her husband. He still did not respond to her voice or touch. Outside she could hear the siren of the ambulance approaching. The flashing lights reflected through the picture window. She ran to the front door and flung it open just as a police car pulled up behind the ambulance. Four medics jumped from the ambulance. Two raced to the back and pulled a gurney onto the street while the other two medics joined Phil Mooney as they raced to the Dutton home.

"Am I glad to see you," Edith exclaimed as she nodded to her husband on the floor beside his chair.

"What happened?" the tallest medic asked as he took a stethoscope from his bag and knelt beside Roy.

"I don't know," Edith murmured. "We were just watching television and when he stood to go to bed he collapsed."

"His heartbeat seems fairly strong and regular," the same medic observed. He then turned to his colleagues who had just appeared with the stretcher. "We need to get him to the hospital right away."

Phil Mooney put a comforting arm on Edith's shoulder.

"Put your coat on and I'll take you to the hospital in the police car."

While the medics were loading Roy into the ambulance, Edith grabbed her coat and purse, flipped off the lights, and locked the door behind her. Phil took her arm as they hurried to the patrol car. Edith's face flushed with worry and excitement as her heart pounded in her chest.

"Phil, would you see that Bob and Jean are notified that they are taking Roy to the hospital?" Edith begged.

"Certainly," Phil responded as he reached for the car radio and called his dispatcher.

"I'm accompanying the ambulance to Rocky Bluff Community Hospital. Would you notify Bob Harkness and Mrs. James Thompson of Running Butte that Roy Dutton collapsed in his home and is on the way to the hospital?"

"Consider it done," the voice replied over the radio. "I hope Roy will be okay."

When the ambulance pulled into the emergency entrance with the patrol car right behind it, Edith could see Doctor Brewer's tall, lean form hurrying across the parking lot.

"What happened?" he asked as he accompanied the gurney through the automatic doors.

Edith again relayed the same story as before as they steered her husband toward examining room number three. "Why don't you wait here in the lobby while we examine Roy?" Doctor Brewer said as he pointed to the familiar emergency waiting room. "The receptionist will get a cup of coffee for you."

Lieutenant Mooney remained in the waiting room with Edith until Bob and Nancy hurried into the hospital twenty minutes later and then he quietly slipped out the side door.

"How's Roy doing?" Bob asked.

"Not well," Edith sighed. Wrinkles increased on her forehead. "I think they've ruled out a heart attack. They are now trying to get the staff and equipment ready to do a CAT scan."

"Mom, how are you holding up?" Nancy queried as she noticed the flush in her cheeks.

Edith took a deep breath. "I haven't had time to think about myself. I've been so worried about Roy. He has suffered enough with his diabetes, he doesn't need anything else."

Edith, Bob, and Nancy watched nervously as the staff bustled in and out of the third emergency room.

"Have you talked with Jean, yet?" Edith murmured.

"They're on their way," Bob assured her. "They're going to drop Gloria off at our house so Dawn can baby-sit. I think it's going to be a long night."

As they sat quietly in the emergency waiting room, Edith's mind drifted back through the different crises that brought their family together in this very place. . . the death of her first husband, George. . . her own heart attack. . . the car accident that killed Roy's son and injured Bob. . . Roy's coming down with diabetes. . . and now this.

"We're very fortunate to have such a good hospital and professional staff," she commented as a nurse hurried by with more supplies. "Many smaller communities in Montana are not able to support a hospital nor keep doctors, while we seem to have one of the best facilities in the area."

Nancy nodded in agreement. "I'll admit we do have one of the finest. Not very many towns have a doctor as concerned about his patients as Doctor Brewer. With his skills I'm sure he could make it big in any large city, yet he chose to treat families in a small town in Montana."

"Quality of life is something money can't buy," Bob replied. "I had to learn that the hard way."

As Bob stood to get another cup of coffee he saw his sister and her husband coming down the corridor. He hurried to meet them. Giving his sister a quick hug he pulled her aside where his mother could not see them.

"Hi, I'm glad you made it," he said with a forced smile. "They are doing a CAT scan right now on Roy. It doesn't look good. I'm also concerned about Mother. Her face is awfully flushed, but she won't consider being checked until she knows how Roy is. I hope your medical background can help console her. She's been through so much."

"I'll do my best," Jean replied as they turned the corner to the waiting room.

"Hello, Mom," Jean said as she leaned over and embraced her weary mother. "How's it going?"

"Not good, I'm afraid," Edith sighed. "We should be hearing the results of the CAT scan soon."

Edith repeated the events of the last few hours while Jean listened attentively. It was easier to explain medical symptoms to her daughter than anyone else.

"It sounds like a stroke to me," Jean said hesitantly. "It will be interesting to see what the scan shows."

Just then Doctor Brewer emerged from the emergency room and approached the family. His eyes immediately rested on Jean. "Hi, Jean, I'm glad you could get here so quick. Roy is going to need all the support he can get."

"How is he?" Jean asked as she scrutinized the doctor's expressions.

"I'm afraid he had an aneurysm that burst," Doctor Brewer replied. "There is a good chance that surgery will improve his chances, but we can't guarantee anything."

Edith's flushed face turned ashen. "Are you sure he's going to make it?"

"Probably so," the doctor explained her. " His heart is still strong, and that's in his favor. However, we don't know how much damage has been done to the brain."

Doctor Brewer paused to give time for the prognosis to settle over the worried family. He sat down in the chair next to Edith and took her hand. "If we do surgery I'll need your permission."

"What's the prognosis without surgery?" Edith queried.

"Not good," Doctor Brewer replied. "There's a chance he might not even regain consciousness."

"Then what is the prognosis with surgery?" Edith continued to question.

"Surgery at his age and with diabetes is risky, but there's hope that he'll be able to have at least partial recovery."

Edith studied the faces of her grown children. They both nodded their heads affirmatively. "Then let's go ahead with the surgery and trust God to protect him."

"That's a wise decision," Doctor Brewer replied. "We'll schedule the surgery for ten o'clock in the morning. We're going to be moving him to intensive care now if you would like to see him for just a few minutes."

The doctor studied Edith's weary face and then continued. "I'd suggest you go home and get some rest. It's going to be a long day tomorrow." He rose and turned his attention back to the entire family. "I'll see you all tomorrow. Good night, now."

Jean was first to take control of the family crisis. "Mom, Jim and I will spend the night with you while Gloria can stay at Bob's. I'm sure she's asleep by now. It's fortunate that tomorrow is Saturday so Dawn will be home to watch her."

That night Edith tossed and turned in her bed from excess caffeine and worry. She tried lying crossways in the bed so she would not be as conscious of the emptiness, but nothing could lift her loneliness and concern. *Will I every be able to share this bed with Roy again? He brought so much meaning and joy into my life.*

The next morning Edith bathed and dressed, then joined Jean and Jim in the kitchen where Jean had prepared a hearty breakfast of hot cereal, fruit and toast.

"You better eat well," Jean reminded her mother. "Who knows how long it will be before we'll be able to eat again."

"I'm really not hungry, but I better have something to keep my strength up," Edith replied. "Roy needs me more than ever now."

Just then the phone rang. The three exchanged nervous glances. "I hope it's not the hospital calling," Jean said as she reached for the phone.

"Hello, this is the Dutton residence. Jean Thompson speaking."

"Hi, Jean. This is Beth Slater. I'm surprised to hear you at your mother's home so early in the morning."

"We came in late last night," Jean explained. "Roy had a stroke last night and is scheduled for surgery at ten this morning."

There was a long silence on the other end of the phone line. "I'm sorry to hear that," Beth faltered. "If there's anything I can do please let me know."

"Prayer is the main thing," Jean reminded her.

Beth's voice quivered. "If I can find someone to stay with Jeffey, do you think it would be okay if I came to the hospital and sat with Edith during the surgery?"

"I'm sure she'll appreciate that."

"Edith always stood by me during all my troubled times, the least I can do is to be there during her difficult times. She and Roy have taught me so much about love."

"We will be leaving for the hospital in fifteen minutes. If you'd like to join us, please do, we'd all enjoy seeing you again," Jean replied. "You've been such a vital part of their lives."

The two visited for a few moments about Roy's condition and then hung up the phone, agreeing to see each other within an hour.

Edith, Jean and Jim arrived at the hospital just as the staff was preparing Roy for surgery. Tears filled Edith's eyes as she watched them shave his distinguished gray hair. "I love you, Roy," she whispered as she took his limp hand. "Hang in there. We'll all be praying for you." She leaned over and kissed his lips and then stepped back so the orderlies could lift him onto the cart and take him to the operating room. Everything was right on schedule as Doctor Brewer had promised the night before.

Within minutes Bob and Nancy joined the rest of the family in the family lounge. "I brought some knitting along to keep my hands busy," Nancy said after greeting her in-laws. "It helps the time go faster for me."

"That's a good idea," Edith replied, "but I'm so nervous now I don't think I could even sign my name."

Nancy reached into her knitting bag. "In that case, I stopped and bought some new magazines for you to look through. The ones in the hospital are always months old."

"Thanks, Nancy," Edith replied. "You always think of everything."

Minutes later Beth Slater walked into the family lounge. She immediately went to Edith and embraced her. "I'm so sorry about Roy. You both mean so much to me."

Edith's voice was weak and tired. "You've brought a great deal of joy into our lives as well."

"Your mature love and marriage is an example for everyone," Beth continued. "You weren't afraid to take a risk with a relationship even though you had to overcome many obstacles. You stood beside each other through both sickness and health."

Edith smiled. "Those words have much more depth than when they are recited at a young couple's wedding ceremony. They are the confidence that love provides, knowing your spouse will be there no matter what happens. The human body can withstand a lot of physical pain if the person knows they are loved unconditionally. That's what mature love is all about."

Beth smiled. "That's what I want in my life as well," she said as she took Edith's hand. "Because of the love I've seen between you and Roy, in spite of all the difficulties you've faced, I'm not afraid to say 'Yes' to Dan's proposal. With God's help we too can promise 'in sickness and health'."

twelve

The minutes ticked by slowly as the friends and family of
Roy Dutton huddled together in the family lounge of the
Rocky Bluff Community Hospital. Nancy busied herself
with her knitting and found that she was having to undo as
much as she was doing, but it helped pass the tense hours
during the surgery. Beth Slater turned the pages of the
magazines, but was unable to concentrate on reading. Only
Edith appeared relatively composed.

Beth studied her older friend's face with bewilderment.
"Edith, how can you appear so calm when the life of the
man you love is on the line?"

Edith chuckled softly. "You should have seen me last
night," she confessed. "I was a nervous wreck."

"She's not kidding," Jean teased. "I was afraid we were
going to have to get a hospital room for her as well."

"I tossed and turned most of the night. Roy and I have
been so happy together these last four years, I didn't want
to lose him," Edith explained. "While I was sitting here
this morning a peace settled over me and instead of becoming angry about Roy's illness, I became thankful for
the four years we have had together. I have completely put
his life in God's hands."

"That takes a lot of courage," Beth replied. "I only wish
my faith were as strong."

Edith patted the young woman's hand. "God doesn't
provide the strength until you need it. This morning I
accepted the fact that if he goes to be with the Lord now it

will be alright. He will no longer be in pain. He has been talking more and more lately about how beautiful heaven must be. I know that we'll have eternity to be together. However, I want to keep him with me for as long as possible. He's added so much joy to my life."

Everyone in the room exchanged looks of embarrassment. Here they were supposed to be comforting Edith and yet she was the one consoling them.

Just then Pastor Rhodes stepped into the room. He nodded to each of the family members and then turned to Edith. "How's it going?"

"The last word from the operating room is that the surgery is going well," Edith responded. "But we won't know for several days how much damage has been done. There's a good chance of paralysis."

"We know he's in God's hands," Pastor Rhodes reminded them. "The church prayer chain is praying for all of you right now. God has been faithful to your family through many crises and He's not going to let you down this time."

"Mother's the pillar of us all," Jean responded. "She's the first one to accept the fact that whatever happens will be God's will."

"Honey, don't make me out to be the saint I'm not," Edith chided. "You saw how I was last night."

All eyes shifted as Doctor Brewer appeared in the doorway. "The surgery went well. The aneurysm was tied off and the blood clot was removed. However, there seems to have been some leakage into the brain. We won't know for several days if there will be any paralysis, but judging by where the leakage occurred, I'm fairly certain the right side of his body will be affected somewhat."

"When can I see him?" Edith pleaded.

"He'll be in the recovery room for about an hour and then they'll move him to intensive care where you can see him for only five minutes every hour," Doctor Brewer explained. "Why don't you get a bite to eat in the hospital cafeteria? The food there is pretty good."

"Thanks so much for all you've done," Edith said as she shook the doctor's hand. "I don't know where our family would be without your excellent care and concern. Rocky Bluff is fortunate to have you."

After Doctor Brewer bid them farewell and returned to the doctors' lounge where he changed into street clothes, Pastor Rhodes smiled and turned to Edith. "We can thank God that the surgery went well and continue to pray for Roy's complete recovery."

"Thank you for coming, Pastor," Edith replied. "I appreciate your concern."

Beth likewise said good-bye as the Harkness family headed for the hospital dining room. Their mood lightened as they each selected their favorite sandwich and soup. Together they had survived another family crisis.

An hour later Edith slipped into Roy's intensive care unit and took his limp hand. His eyes slowly opened. "Hello, Roy," she whispered. "How are you doing?"

A faint smile spread across his face. The muscles around his face began to twitch. "He. . . he. . . he. . . lo," he stammered. "I. . . I. . . I'm. . . s. . . s. . . slee. . . py." Roy closed his eyes and faded into a deep slumber.

Edith leaned over and kissed him on the forehead and slipped out of the room to join her waiting family. "Jean, I know it's too early to tell for sure, but I'm afraid his speech is going to be impaired. He had a lot of trouble forming his words."

"That's fairly common after all that he's been through," Jean explained. "It could be that the anesthetics have not worn off."

"But this was different from slurred, drugged speech,"

Edith persisted. "He tried so hard to communicate with me, but he wasn't able to make the sounds."

One by one the other family members slipped into Roy's room, but he did not rouse. As Jean slipped out of the room, Edith looked wearily at her daughter. "Would you mind taking me home? Now that I know Roy is okay I think I could sleep for a week."

"That's a good idea. We could all use a good nap."

Edith slept most of that afternoon. Jean fixed her mother's favorite dish for dinner. . . spaghetti and meatballs. As soon as she had finished eating, Edith went back to bed and slept the entire night. Every cell in her body seemed to be craving complete rest.

By eight o'clock the next morning Edith was dressed and in the kitchen preparing breakfast for Jean and Jim. Jean stumbled into the kitchen in her bathrobe with her hair tousled. "Mother, you shouldn't have to fix breakfast for us," she protested. "Give me a few minutes and I'll have breakfast on the table."

"I need to make myself useful sometime," Edith teased. "Besides, I'm anxious to get to the hospital and see Roy. He should be alert today."

"Well, if you insist," Jean replied with a twinkle in her eye. "We'll be with you in just a few minutes. Jim is finishing showering now."

An hour later Edith, Jean, and Jim stopped at the nurses' station at intensive care.

"Hello, Edith," the nurse greeted. "How are you today?"

"I'm fine," she replied. "How is Roy doing?"

"He rested well," the nurse replied. "But he seems to have some paralysis on his right side and his speech is slurred. I'm sure Doctor Brewer will want to talk to you about physiotherapy as soon as Roy is strong enough. His body has suffered an awful shock and since he's a diabetic it will take even longer for him to heal."

"I'm so thankful he's pulling through the operation," Edith sighed. "When he left the house in the ambulance I wasn't sure of anything."

"I'll admit it was kind of touch and go for a while," the supervising nurse explained. "But Roy has a tough constitution and a strong will to live. Others would have given up under much less difficulties."

Edith eyed the door to her husband's room. "May I see him now?"

"I'm sure he'll enjoy it. Just remember he's only allowed one visitor at a time for only five minutes."

As Edith opened the door, Roy's face broke into a broad grin. "H. . . h. . . h. . . i, E. . . E. . . d. . . d. . . ith," he stammered.

Edith took her husband's hand as she leaned over to kiss him. "How are you doing?" she whispered.

"F. . . f. . . f. . . i. . . i. . . ne. . . .."

"That's good," she whispered, trying to mask the lump in her throat. "We'll have you up and running in no time."

"C. . . c. . . c. . . a. . . n. . . n. . . t   m. . . m. . . o. . . v. . . ve."

"There's all kinds of gadgets to help," Edith reminded him gently. "Doctor Brewer is probably planning a pretty extensive workout for you. Are you up to it?"

Roy grinned and nodded his head affirmatively.

"That's the spirit," Edith replied. "You'll have to show the world that one's never too old to keep fighting for the good life."

Roy squeezed Edith's hand as he smiled.

"Jean and Jim are anxious to see you," Edith explained. "They came down late Friday night, but Jim has to be in Running Butte by early morning. They're expecting a big shipment for the new store, but he'll be by later today to see you."

Roy nodded his head affirmatively.

"They're really protecting you now," Edith teased. "They'll only let one of us in at a time so I better go now so everyone else can see you before they leave. I love you."

"I. . . l. . . l. . . l. . . o. . . v. . . ve. . . y. . . y. . . y. . . ou."

After watching how Roy struggled to form each letter, Jean had a running monologue explaining the progress of the Running Butte Crisis Center. She could sense his intense interest by the sparkle in his eyes. Roy was trapped in a body that was unable to communicate with his loved ones.

While Edith was waiting in the hallway in front of her husband's room, Dan Blair, Beth Slater, and Jeffey entered. "We had to come and see how Roy's doing before we go to church," Dan explained. "I was shocked to hear what happened. Roy seemed to be doing so well lately."

Edith shook her head. "One never knows when something like this is going to happen. He had one close call."

"If there is anything I can do to help, please feel free to ask," Dan stated. "Will you be needing transportation to the hospital or anything like that?"

Edith's eyes brightened. "Jean and Jim are going home this afternoon and, of course, Bob and Nancy work all day, so I'll be needing rides to the hospital until Roy's released."

"Consider it done," Dan replied. "Just tell me what time you'd like a ride and I'll be there."

"Would ten o'clock every day be too much of an inconvenience?" Edith replied. "I feel like a terrible burden since I haven't been able to drive myself after my heart attack."

"No problem at all," Dan assured her. "There are some advantages of working the night shift."

The days passed slowly for Edith. Promptly at ten o'clock

each day Dan took her to the hospital and then returned to get her at three. Edith did her best to keep Roy's spirits high and chatted about the grandchildren, school, church activities, and the progress of the new hardware store.

Three weeks after Roy's stroke, Doctor Brewer invited Edith to join him in the family lounge. "Edith," he began cautiously. "This is very difficult for me to say, but the restoration of Roy's functions are not going as easy as I'd like. Through physical therapy he is beginning to get some range of motion in his right leg and arm, but he is far from being able to walk and feed himself. I think it's time we begin considering other options."

Edith's chin dropped. "What options are left? I would really like to bring him home, but I won't be able to care for him in the condition he's in now."

"Edith, Roy is going to need physiotherapy and specialized health services for a long time and strong backs that will be able to lift him from his bed to his chair. My advice is to place him in a long-term skilled nursing facility," Doctor Brewer replied gently.

Edith sat in stunned silence. "You mean he'll have to be in a nursing home?" she murmured.

"I'm afraid so," Doctor Brewer responded. "People often think placing a family member in a nursing home is a sign of self-centeredness and cruelty when in reality it can be the kindest thing you can do for your loved one."

"But I promised before God that we'd be together until 'death do us part'," Edith protested with tears in her eyes.

Doctor Brewer took Edith's hand. "Just because Roy's in a nursing home does not mean you'll have to abandon him." He paused before continuing. "We have a fine facility right here in Rocky Bluff. You could visit him every day and even make arrangements to have your meals together in the dining room with the others."

Edith shuddered at the thought of nightly separation from her beloved husband. "The house is so lonely without him. It would not only be an adjustment for him but also for me."

"With the nursing home connected to the hospital Roy will be able to continue his daily physical therapy treatments," Doctor Brewer explained. "If he ever becomes able to walk and take care of himself, I'll be the first one to recommend him returning to his own home."

Edith thought back through the years of the times she visited the nursing home with either a church group, a school group, or just to visit an elderly friend. "There is one advantage to a nursing home in a smaller community over one in the city," she noted.

"And what is that?" Doctor Brewer queried.

"There is a lot of community involvement in the activities of the home. The program coordinator generally has something different going on every afternoon."

Doctor Brewer nodded with agreement. "That's true. Often the patients have a lot more social activities than when they were alone in their own home."

"That's true for most people," Edith replied, "but Roy always seemed to have a string of friends stopping by the house for a cup of coffee. We've gone through three coffeemakers just in the short time we've been married."

"Then I'm sure Roy won't be lacking in company while he's in the community nursing home." Doctor Brewer gazed out the window at the freshly fallen snow. Helping family members accept the perhaps permanent limitations of a loved one was one of the hardest parts of his job as family doctor. "Edith, should I go ahead and make arrangements with the director to have Roy transferred as soon as the next bed is available?"

"Could I have a couple days to talk with my family?" Edith queried. "I don't want to make such a big decision without first consulting them."

"Of course," Doctor Brewer responded. "We probably won't need a decision until the end of the week. Would you call me by Friday and let me know what you've decided?"

"Sure," she responded. "I just want to make certain I'm doing the right thing for Roy."

That afternoon Edith rode home in silence, lost in her own thoughts. Dan Blair had long since learned that there comes a time when people need to be alone to sort through their own feelings and did not pressure her for details. As soon as she walked in her home, Edith hung up her coat and went directly to the phone.

"Hello, Jean," she said when her daughter's voice echoed through the receiver.

"Hello, Mom. How are you doing?"

"I'm fine. How are you and Gloria?"

"We're doing great. We're as busy as we can be with the new medical center being so close to completion. How's Roy?"

"That's what I'm calling about," Edith confessed. "Would you and Jim mind driving to Rocky Bluff tomorrow night? I want to get the entire family together and discuss his condition."

"No problem," Jean replied, sensing the concern in her mother's voice. "In fact, I'll come down early enough to make a big dinner for our family."

ᕥ

The next afternoon when Dan dropped Edith at home after her daily visit to the hospital, she found Jean busy in her kitchen. She gazed around the counters and smelled the ham cooking in the oven. "This is going to be better than a Christmas dinner the way you're going at this," she teased.

"Any day is a good day to make special," Jean replied as she finished tossing the salad. "Besides Jay and Dawn were going to come and I don't want them to think I've lost my touch."

"I'm glad they're going to be here," Edith replied. "Those two are extremely mature for their years."

The Harkness family chattered back and forth about the routine issues of daily life in Rocky Bluff, each knowing that something important was to be decided, but the dinner table was not the time nor the place to address it. After everyone had finished dinner and Jean and Dawn had loaded the dishwasher, the entire family gathered in Edith's living room. All eyes settled on her. Now was the time.

Edith cleared her throat as she surveyed her family. "I had a long talk with Doctor Brewer yesterday," she began. "He said that Roy's rehabilitation is not coming along as well as he'd like and that we need to consider other options."

Jean studied her mother's face. "Is he suggesting we put Roy in a nursing home?"

"Exactly. He felt Roy needs intense physical therapy and specialized care that we can't provide at home."

Tears filled Dawn's eyes. "But he can't go to the nursing home. He needs to be at home so we can visit him all the time," the thirteen-year-old protested. "Jean's a nurse, couldn't she care for him the way she took care of you after your heart attack?"

Jean put her arm around her niece. "I wish it were that simple," she sighed, "but Roy's medical problems are much different from what your grandmother experienced. Roy is not able to walk, so two strong people will have to lift him every time he needs to get out of bed or go to the bathroom. I'm not strong enough to do that alone."

"Also, Dawn," Edith continued. "Roy has to have physical therapy everyday so he can learn to reuse his right arm and leg. We wouldn't have any way to get him back and forth from the hospital from here."

"It just seems so mean to put him in the nursing home," Jay protested.

"I felt the same way until Doctor Brewer talked to me," Edith confided. "Now I feel like it's the kindest thing I can do under the circumstances. He told me I can have my meals in the dining room with Roy everyday so it won't be like we're abandoning him. Even if he can't talk to communicate, we are still spiritually one."

"We can all visit him regularly," Bob stated. "He's done so much for us that's it's time we give something back. I know it's hard when he can't talk the way he'd like, but he still talks with his eyes and with time he can get a few words out."

Finally, the wisdom of specialized care became a reality for Dawn. "The nursing home isn't that far out of my way home from school," she noted. "I can stop by nearly every evening and bring my friends with me."

"We want to let the entire world know how much we love our grandpa and make him the most visited resident in the home," Jay inserted.

"Then everyone is in agreement that I should let Doctor Brewer go ahead and make the transfer to the nursing home?" Edith queried.

Everyone shook their head affirmatively.

"Thanks," Edith smiled. "You've made this decision so much easier for me. It's comforting to know that when problems arise we can always stand together as a family."

thirteen

"Beth, did you notice how Roy looked at Edith today while she was reading to him? He may not be able to verbally communicate well, but his eyes spoke volumes," Dan said as the young couple relaxed in Beth's living room after Jeffey was in bed.

Beth's voice softened. "Their devotion is an inspiration of the faithfulness of love, even through the toughest times."

Dan put his arm around Beth. "The more I see the fruits of their marriage the more I want to experience some of the same benefits with you," he implored. "Beth, when will I get an answer to my proposal?"

"Tonight," she whispered as she laid her head on his chest. "I feel just the way you do. After seeing Roy and Edith's love through the most difficult of times, I'm no longer afraid to love someone unconditionally."

The young couple embraced with ecstasy. Never had either one of them been happier. Love rushed into the empty hole in both their lives. "Honey, I'm am so happy every time I'm with you," Dan murmured into her ear. "Let's set a wedding date for as soon as possible."

Beth pulled back from their embrace. "There's so much going on now and it will take several months to make wedding plans," she protested good-naturedly. "I couldn't possibly be ready until after school is out in June."

"Then June it is," Dan declared. "Saturday let's go down to Rothstein's Jewelry Store and pick out the biggest diamond we can afford."

Beth gasped. "A diamond? I never expected a real diamond. Aren't we being frivolous when there's so many bills to pay?"

"Diamonds are an investment, not a luxury. You deserve the very best. Our love is forever."

Beth hugged her fiancee with delight. "Dan, I love you so much. I never knew life could be so good."

"If you can find someone to watch Jeffey, I'll pick you up at one o'clock Saturday."

"I don't think that'll be a problem," Beth replied. "Several girls at school nearly beg to baby-sit him."

"Great," Dan nearly shouted with exhilaration. "Saturday after I take Edith to the nursing home I'll come and take you downtown. Be sure and circle that day on the calendar in red."

Saturday afternoon found Dan and Beth perched on two bar stools in front of the diamond case of Rothstein's Jeweler's. "Which one do you like the best?" Dan asked as they peered through the glass.

"I don't know what to say. They're all beautiful."

"Do you like a round or an emerald cut?" the jeweler asked as he took an example of each from the show case.

"I like that one best," Beth replied as she pointed to a one-half karat solitaire.

"Try it on and see how it looks," Dan begged.

Beth slid the ring onto her third finger, left hand. "It's beautiful," she gasped. "I can't wear something like this all the time."

"Of course you can," Dan reminded her as he pointed to a bridal set in the back corner of the diamond case. "Why don't you try that one."

The jeweler took out the bridal set Dan selected and helped Beth slide it onto her finger. The solitaire engagement ring was accented by the swirl of smaller diamonds of the wedding band encircling it.

Beth gasped, "I've never seen anything as exquisite as this."

Dan turned to the jeweler. "We'll take this one."

Beth handed the set back to the jeweler who placed it in its box. "Will it be cash or charge?" he asked Dan.

"I'll write a check," Dan responded proudly. "I've been saving for this day for a long time."

"But we only agreed to marry this week," Beth teased suspiciously.

"I had you picked out a long time ago," Dan laughed. "I knew it would just be a matter of time before you came around."

"Fortunately, Beth's ring size is a perfect six, the same as most of the bridal sets are initially manufactured, so there won't be a need to size them. You can take them with you now if you'd like," the jeweler explained.

Dan wrote the check while the jeweler filled out the guarantee papers. The transaction was soon completed and the happy couple walked out the door holding hands. As soon as they were inside the car, Dan took the little box from his pocket.

"Beth, I can't wait to have you begin wearing this," he said as he held out the engagement ring. "I want to shout it to the world that you have agreed to be Mrs. Dan Blair."

Dan slid the ring onto her finger. Forgetting the passersby on the sidewalk, their lips met for a lasting moment. Soon they would be one family.

"I can't believe this is happening," Beth exclaimed. "I

want to shout it to the world."

"Let's go by the nursing home and show the ring to Roy and Edith," Dan replied eagerly. "Without them I don't think any of this would have been possible."

Beth squeezed his hand as Dan reached for the ignition. Rarely did she have trouble finding something to talk about, but the excitement of this moment left her speechless. Dan parked his car in front of the Care Center and hurried inside. They found Edith in Roy's room reading the *Herald* to him.

Seeing the young couple, Roy broke into a broad grin. "H. . . H. . . He. . . l. . . l. . . lo, D. . . D. . . D. . . an."

"Hi, Roy. You're looking good today," Dan greeted as he shook his hand. "Hello, Edith. How's it going for the both of you?"

"Really good," Edith replied. "Roy is getting the best of care here. And, believe it or not, the food here is really good. I am so grateful that you're able to bring me over every day so I can have lunch with him."

"I enjoy doing it," Dan replied as he pulled up chairs for himself and Beth. He looked over at his fiancee and lifted her left hand. The diamond flashed in the sunlight that streaked through the window.

Edith took Beth's hand from Dan. "Beth, that's beautiful. Congratulations," she exclaimed. "I'm so happy for you."

Beth beamed. "I never thought anything like this could ever happen to me. I feel like a princess being swept away by my prince charming."

Roy reached for Beth's left hand. He smiled as he gazed at the diamond and then lifted her hand to his lips in a form of blessing. Being mute didn't not prevent him from communicating his true feelings.

"Have you set the date yet?" Edith queried.

"I'm awfully busy until school is out," Beth replied, "but hopefully we can get married in June so we have the entire summer together before I have to go back to work."

"We haven't talked with Pastor Rhodes, yet," Dan inserted. "I hope our wedding won't interfere with his vacation."

"I doubt it," Edith replied. "He usually takes his family on vacation late in the summer."

Beth glanced at Roy. His chin had sunk against his chest and his eyes had closed. "Looks like it's afternoon nap time," she whispered.

Edith smiled. "Dan, would you mind taking me home now? I think Roy's had enough excitement for the day. Seeing the two of you so happy will give him pleasure for days to come."

The next day Dan, Beth, and little Jeffey lingered behind the rest of the congregation so they could speak with Pastor Rhodes a few moments privately. "Dan. . . Beth, you both look extremely radiant today," Pastor Rhodes greeted.

"We have a reason to be," Dan chuckled. "Beth has agreed to marry me," he said as he lifted Beth's left hand.

"Congratulations," the pastor smiled. "That is a beautiful ring."

"We were wondering if there would be a weekend in June in which you could perform the ceremony for us?"

Pastor Rhodes took his black schedule book from his coat pocket. "It looks like the last three weekends are open so you can have your pick of dates. I like to have at least four premarital counseling sessions with the engaged couple before the ceremony. Could we set up a time this week to get together and discuss the details?"

Dan looked at Beth. They were already beginning to think as one. "With our strange work schedules, Saturdays seem to be the best time for both of us," Dan told the pastor.

Pastor Rhodes flipped a couple pages in his schedule book. "How does two o'clock in my office sound?"

"We'll be there," Dan promised as he took Beth's hand in his right and Jeffey's in his left.

That is a mighty promising family in the making, Pastor Rhodes mused as the three walked happily down the front steps of the church.

It did not take long the next morning for word to spread through the faculty and students of Rocky Bluff High School that the library clerk had just become engaged and was sporting a new diamond. The teenage girls rushed to the library as soon as they had a break between classes. Beth could scarcely get her books shelved for the day.

"Miss Slater, let me see your ring."

"It's beautiful."

"Are you going to invite us to your wedding?"

"I wish my boyfriend would give me a diamond like that."

At lunch time Beth was surrounded by well-wishing faculty members. Beth scarcely knew how to respond to their enthusiasm. The most enthusiastic of all was the librarian Rebecca Sutherland.

"Beth," she exclaimed over cafeteria hamburger. "We're going to have to throw a big shower in celebration. It's not often we get to help start one of our own out on a voyage of marital bliss."

The entire faculty lounge burst into gales of laughter.

"Men's dirty socks stuck under the bed," one teacher chided.

"Caps left off the toothpaste," added another.

"Someone drinking directly out of a milk carton instead of using a glass," laughed another.

Beth blushed. "I don't know what to say. It's all so exciting. Even if I have to reach under the bed to find the dirty socks," she teased back.

"Consider the formation of the shower committee made and invitations for a party sometime in May will be forthcoming," Rebecca said just as the bell rang summoning them back to class.

The next Saturday afternoon Beth and Dan arrived at Pastor Rhodes's office promptly at two o'clock. After exchanging pleasantries, the first thing on the agenda was to select a wedding date. With little discussion, June twenty-first was written on the church calendar.

Pastor Rhodes then looked at the future bride across the room from him. "Beth, your entire countenance has changed since you became engaged."

"There's a good reason," Beth beamed. "I'm happier than I've ever been in my life. After all I've done in my life I feel like I don't deserve all this, but yet good things keep happening to me."

Pastor Rhodes became serious. "Jesus not only died for what you've done in the past," he assured her. "He also came that you might have life and have it abundantly."

Beth grinned. "Well, having Dan's love is definitely making my life abundant."

"How's Jeffey accepting the idea of you getting married?" Pastor Rhodes asked. "After all, he's had your undivided attention all his life."

"Jeffey's excited that he's finally going to have a daddy," Beth responded. "He thinks the world of Dan."

"I've noticed that in church," Pastor Rhodes responded.

"He spends a lot of time sitting on your lap or holding your hand."

"I'd like to adopt him if it's at all possible," Dan stated. "But I don't know where to begin since his natural father is in jail in Canada."

"Why don't you talk with Stuart Leonard about that?" the pastor suggested. "He'll probably be able to help you out. He's already familiar with the law enforcement agencies in Canada after he worked to get Jeffey released back to Montana last fall."

"Dan, I wish you would talk to Stu as soon as possible," Beth pleaded. "Jeffey's adoption would make us truly a traditional family. . . something I thought I would never have because of my stupidity with Mickey."

"I'll call him Monday and make an appointment," Dan assured her as he took her hand. "Jeffey is already so much like a son to me that I want to make it official at the same time I make you my wife."

Pastor Rhodes directed the remaining conversation toward the characteristics of a Christian marriage and some common pitfalls that might befall them. Both Dan and Beth were eager to begin their married life with a firm commitment that together they could conquer anything.

The following Wednesday afternoon Dan greeted Pat as he entered the Little Big Horn County Attorney's office.

"Hello, Dan. It's good to see you," the secretary greeted. "Won't you be seated. Stu will be right with you."

Just then the distinguished county attorney appeared in the doorway. "Dan, how are you doing?" he said as he extended his right hand. "Won't you come into my office?"

Stu motioned for Dan to be seated in a chair to the right

of his desk. "What can I do to help you today?" he queried.

Dan took a deep breath. "I suppose you know that Beth
and I are getting married in June."

"In Rocky Bluff there are no secrets," the attorney chuckled.

"Well, I was wondering what my chances would be to
adopt Jeffey?"

"It's within the realm of possibilities," Stu replied. "It
mainly depends on if the natural father would sign a waiver
giving up his rights as a father."

"Since he's in jail in Canada wouldn't that be pretty hard
to do?"

Stu surveyed the earnest young man's intense expression. "Not necessarily. We do have several things in our
advantage. First, we know exactly where he is and second
we also know his attorney. I can draw up the papers and
call Greg McIntyre in Calgary and see if he will go to the
jail and ask Mickey to waive his paternal rights."

"After all the trouble he went to in kidnapping Jeffey
and taking him to Canada, I doubt if he'd sign anything,"
Dan said dejectedly.

"I don't think Mickey's behavior was caused by any
paternal instinct. He only wanted revenge on Beth and a
cover for his criminal activities. If he thought he'd have to
pay child support just as soon as he returned to the States,
I think he might be glad to have someone else take over his
responsibilities. Give me a few days to work on it."

"Thank you so much," Dan said as he rose to leave.
"I'd like to make Jeffey my son at the same time as I make
his mother my wife."

"I'll be in touch with you in a couple of days after I've

talked with Greg McIntyre. I think we have a good shot at this one."

છે

The next few weeks flew by for Beth and Dan as they made plans for their upcoming wedding and honeymoon. There were bridesmaids' dresses and a bridal dress to order. . . flowers. . . invitations. . . food. . . showers. Beth was astir with all the excitement, but she had the best advisor possible in planning a social occasion, the former home economics teacher, Edith Dutton.

છે

"Mickey, you have company," the prison guard said as he unlocked the cell and motioned for him to walk down the corridor toward the visitor's room.

"Who is it?"

"I think it's your attorney."

Mickey smiled as he sat at the table and peered through the mesh separating the prisoner from the guest.

"Hi, Greg, did you come to get me out of here?"

"You don't have a chance for parole for several more months," the attorney stated flatly. "However, I do have a proposition for you to consider."

"What's that?"

"Beth Slater is planning to get married in June and her fiancé, Dan Blair, would like to adopt Jeffey. They need you to sign a waiver giving up your parental rights."

"I'm not going to do that," Mickey sneered. "He's my kid."

"That's right, Mickey, he is," Greg McIntyre replied. "However, since he's your child you're responsible for child support payments under United States law. As soon as you cross the border you'll be expected to pay child support."

"Ah. . . I suppose I could kick in fifty dollars a month if they force me to."

"Child support payments in the States can run five to six hundred dollars a month," Greg explained.

"You mean that as soon as I go home I'll have to pay that much? Even if I did get a decent job I wouldn't be able to support myself and give that much to Jeffey. Besides, Beth will only spend it on herself. She has a good job, she can support him."

"Legally, you're still responsible until Jeffey becomes eighteen."

Mickey sat in silence. "That's a heck of a lot of money. How am I going to get out of this?" he sighed. "If I'm not in a jail with four walls and bars, I'll be in financial jail for the rest of my life."

"You could sign the waiver giving up your parental rights and then Dan would be responsible for paying all his bills."

"If I sign this, as soon as I get out of jail I can go back to the States and I get a job without having anything hanging over my head?"

"Yes, Jeffey will be entirely Dan's and Beth's responsibility."

Mickey's eyes began to moisten. "I've always wanted to go back to Montana as soon as I get out of here. I left the state when I joined the Marines and I don't think I could be happy any other place. Where do I sign?"

fourteen

"Beth, would you and Jeffey like to go to Running Butte with me a week from Saturday?" Dan asked as the pair sat watching TV in Beth's cozy apartment.

"Sure, what's the occasion?"

"Libby Reynolds called today. They've settled into their new double-wide mobile home there and she'd like to have a little housewarming dinner. She asked if we'd be able to bring Edith Dutton with us."

Beth smiled. "That sounds like a good idea. I wished I could have helped them move, but I had to work that day."

"They had plenty of help," Dan assured her. "Since Libby is pregnant, no one would let her lift even the smallest box."

"I am anxious to see their new place. When does the new store open?"

"That Saturday is the grand opening of Harkness Two. That's why she'd like us to bring Edith. Larry and the rest of the Harkness clan are going to be busy at the store all day."

Beth's thoughts drifted back through the months that she had known Libby Reynolds. "So much has happened since Edith introduced me to Libby and I started taking care of her little Vanessa while she went to paralegal school."

"I don't think Rocky Bluff will ever forget the night the Harkness Hardware Store burned down, the arson investigation, and their grand reopening," Dan's face broke into a broad grin. "I know I'll never forget the grand reopening," he said as he put his arm around his fiancee. "That was the day we met."

"It's interesting how a serendipity happens when we're going about our daily routines," Beth sighed as she laid her head upon his chest. "Who would have thought the reopening of a local business would affect me for the rest of my life?"

"That fire had a life changing effect on Larry and Libby as well," Dan replied. "Before that time Libby was a terrified young abused wife calling the crisis line. Within months they were renewing their wedding vows, and here they are now with a new home of their own and another baby on the way."

"Isn't it interesting that here in Rocky Bluff, when people's lives change for the better, somewhere in the background is the influence of Edith Dutton?"

❧

The leaf in Libby's kitchen table extended to include Beth, Dan, Jeffey, and Edith into the Reynolds's family circle.

"I'm glad you could come to our grand opening," Larry said as he passed the mashed potatoes to Edith. "This store is like a miracle springing up in a decaying hamlet. The reservation people are so appreciative of anyone investing in their world."

"I'm looking forward to seeing the store," Edith noted as she looked out the front window and saw cars lining the road for two blocks.

"The store's just packed," Larry continued. "Bob and Nancy, along with Jim and Jean, are really busy. I promised I wouldn't be gone long so they can each take a few minutes to catch a bite to eat."

Edith turned to Libby. "When do they expect to get the new clinic open?"

"They're looking at the middle of June for the construction to be completed. Both the physician's assistant and the new attorney will be moving into Running Butte about that time," Libby explained. "Their grand opening is scheduled for the second week of July."

"How exciting," Beth declared, trying to grasp the enormity of the project. "But isn't that about the time your baby is due?"

A look of pleasure settled across Libby's face. "The exact due date is the fifteenth of June, so it ought to be a busy month for us."

"It's going to be a great month for us as well," Dan chuckled. "I'll be gaining a wife and a son at the same time."

"I sure hope I'm not in the hospital and will be able to come to your wedding," Libby replied. "I hated having to decline being your bridesmaid, but it's not a very good time for me."

"Actually, it's because you won't know what size to make your bridesmaid's dress," Larry chuckled as he patted his wife's tummy.

Libby blushed and then took Vanessa from her high chair before she began clearing the table. "Let me help," Beth said as she began to stack the plates to carry them to the sink.

Within half an hour the small gathering in the Reynolds's kitchen had moved to the new hardware store. Edith's eyes filled with tears as she approached her son. "Bob, you've done an excellent job. Your father would be proud of you. It was always his dream to expand the store to another community, but he never had a chance. That heart attack just came too early for him."

"Mom, we couldn't have done it without you," Bob replied as he hugged his mother. "You've stood behind us through thick and thin."

"There were a lot of times we all felt like we were on pretty thin ice," Edith chuckled. "But fortunately the ice never broke."

"Hi, Grandma. Isn't this store neat?" Dawn exclaimed as she hurried down the aisle leading her cousin Gloria. "I've been helping pour punch and serve cookies. Would you like to have some?"

"I'd love to," Edith replied as she followed her grand-daughter to the serving table where Dan, Beth, and Jeffey had already joined Nancy and Jean.

Jean leaned over and kissed her mother. "Hi, Mom. I'm so glad you could come."

Edith grinned. "I wouldn't miss this for the world. How's it going?"

"Really great," Jean replied, "but I don't know what we would have done without Larry. As soon as they moved here he unboxed the computer system and had everything up and running in no time."

"He's come a long way since he played basketball at Rocky Bluff High School," Edith replied.

Suddenly Jean spotted a friend down a side aisle. "Mother, there's someone I'd like you to meet. Wait a minute and I'll go get him."

Within moments Jean returned followed by a heavy set, middle-aged man wearing two braids that extended past his shoulders. "Mother, I'd like you to meet Chief Joseph Black Hawk. Chief Black Hawk, this is my mother, Edith Dutton."

"It's nice to meet you, Mrs. Dutton. I've heard so many good things about you. Your daughter and son-in-law have been a great asset to our community the few months they've been here. We're all looking forward to not having to spend two and a half hours on the road just to get a simple nut or bolt."

"I'm sure it's been a real trial for you, especially in the winter," Edith replied. "Also, having your own medical and legal center here should help Running Butte develop a sense of self-reliance and encourage their young people to strive for higher goals."

"Jean has worked hand-in-hand with us trying to bring these social services to the local people. She's considered one of our kindred spirits. You should be mighty proud of her."

Edith beamed. "That I am. Her forte has always been to help others, regardless of the personal sacrifice to herself," she replied. "It was very nice meeting you and I hope we'll have a chance to get together again at the grand opening of the new medical clinic."

৵

Rebecca Sutherland was just finishing typing a purchase order when Beth arrived at work Monday morning.

"Good morning, Beth," she greeted. "How was your weekend?"

"Great," Beth replied. "Dan and I took Edith Dutton to the grand opening of Harkness Two in Running Butte Saturday. They really did a good job getting that store set up."

"They are a multitalented family," Rebecca noted. "I enjoyed working with Edith when she was the home economics teacher here. She had so much concern for each individual student whether she had them in class or not."

"Since she's retired Edith seems to have spread that same concern throughout the community," Beth replied as she sat down at the desk opposite Rebecca's.

"Beth, I have some exciting news to tell you," the older woman began. "I've put in twenty-five years in school libraries and I figure it's time for me to make a change."

Beth's heart sank. She'd enjoyed working with Rebecca these last few months. "You're not thinking of retiring are you?"

"Not exactly," Rebecca replied. "But I've received a contract from a private high school in Guam to come for two years and organize their library."

"Guam? Where's that?"

"It's a little island in the Pacific that's one of our U.S. territories. We have both a naval station and an air base there. I heard they needed a lot of help with their educational system so I thought it might be a good place to put my experience to work."

"Sounds exciting, but do they speak English there?" Beth queried as pictures of coconut palms and brown-skinned natives flashed before her.

"Oh, yes," Rebecca grinned. "Everyone speaks English, but most of the natives are bilingual and also speak their local Chamorro language. It's going to be quite a challenge."

The thought of a close friend in a distant land overwhelmed Beth. "When do you plan to leave?"

"Probably the first part of August," Rebecca explained. "I'd like to take a couple weeks to tour the Hawaiian Islands on my way over."

Beth's eyes gleamed. "Lucky you."

"I've been saving for a long time for such a vacation,"

Rebecca responded with a distant gaze in her eyes. "Beth, there's one thing I'd like you and Dan to think about. Maybe it would be advantageous for the both of us."

"What's that?"

"I need to have someone live in my house while I'm gone and take care of general maintenance, plus water my plants and feed and love my Pekinese, Shushu. I could move the furniture you don't want to use to the basement. I want someone who I know and trust to live there while I'm away. I wouldn't charge you any rent."

Beth's eyes widened as she visualized Rebecca's large brick home on the edge of town. "You have such a beautiful home. It's hard to imagine myself living in something that nice. It would be quite a responsibility. I'll talk to Dan and get back to you in a few days. Thanks for the offer."

Beth could hardly wait to see Dan that evening. When he arrived at seven o'clock, she breathlessly told the story of Rebecca's offer. She concluded her monologue with, "But I've never lived in anything like that before. I've always been in awe of people who live in beautiful homes."

Dan smiled. "Behind the fancy homes they're just ordinary people like you and me," he assured her. "There's nothing at all snobbish about Rebecca, is there?"

"No. She's one of the most down-to-earth people I know," Beth agreed. "God just seems to have blessed her with that home and now she's willing to let us live there free for two years."

"This could be a real godsend for us," Dan noted. "For two years we can save the money we'd normally spend for rent and use it toward a down payment on a house of our own."

Beth's eyes became distant. "This is like a fairy tale, just a few months ago I was struggling on welfare and now I'm making plans to become a homeowner," she murmured.

"Then you agree we should take her up on her offer?" Dan queried.

"I'm a little concerned having Jeffey in such a beautiful home. What if he spills something on her plush beige carpet or breaks one of her lamps?"

Dan took her hand to calm her fears. "That could happen to anyone. If it happens we just have the carpet cleaned or replace the lamp. You should be very proud of Jeffey. He's such a well-behaved child."

Beth nodded in agreement. "Okay, then let's go for it. I'll tell her tomorrow that we'll be happy to do it. Then when the time for her to leave gets closer we can get together and discuss the details."

The next day Edith invited Dan into her home for coffee after he brought her home from visiting Roy in the nursing home. Edith poured two cups of coffee and took a half dozen home-baked cookies from the cookie jar before she joined Dan at the kitchen table.

"Roy didn't look as well today," Dan noted as he took his first sip of steaming coffee.

"His color wasn't good at all and his expression seemed blank and distant," Edith sighed as the wrinkles deepened in her forehead. "The head nurse said he had a very restless sleep. They're suspicious that he is having minor strokes, but no one can be sure."

"I admire your persistence in visiting him every day in spite of the weather."

"Roy's body may be wearing out, but as long as he has

breath his gentle spirit will always shine through," Edith
replied. "Have you noticed that despite how miserable he
may feel, he rarely complains?"

"You both have been a real inspiration to Beth and me.
We hope we can demonstrate our love for each other the
way you and Roy have."

"I'm sure you will," Edith assured him. "You both know
what it's like to suffer misfortune and to keep your eyes on
the Lord through the tough times as well as the good times."

Edith's interest in talking about herself and her own problems was short-lived. "How are the wedding plans coming?"

Dan beamed. "Beth has all the wedding details under
control. The gals at the school are throwing a shower for
her next week so she's really busy. She's leaving the big
things to me, like planning a honeymoon and where we're
going to live."

"And where will that be?" Edith queried. "Both your
apartments are too small for three people."

"We'll have to stay at Beth's until the first part of
August. After that Rebecca asked us to house-sit her home
while she's in Guam for two years," Dan explained.

Edith poured Dan another cup of coffee and passed the
plate of cookies to him. "That sounds like a good deal for
the both of you. I'm really excited about Rebecca's contract on Guam. With her experience she'll be able to build
an outstanding library for them."

"It's an opportunity of a lifetime for her," Dan agreed.
"I hope someday Beth and I will be able to travel abroad."

Edith smiled. "It's hard to know what bend in the road
our lives will take," she replied. "Life changing events
happen when we least expect them."

Later that afternoon when Dan returned to his apartment the phone rang. "Hello."

"Hello, Dan. This is Stuart Leonard."

"Oh, hi, Stu. Any word yet?"

"That's why I'm calling," the county attorney replied. "I just got word from Greg McIntyre in Calgary. He said that Mickey Kilmer signed the papers surrendering his paternal rights, so you're free to adopt Jeffey."

Dan's eyes filled with tears. "I don't know how to thank you. Now what do I do next?"

"Now it's time to hire an attorney," Stu explained. "I'd like to help, but as county attorney I can't engage in private practice."

"Yes, I know. There are a couple of attorneys in town I could call. Thanks so much for your help," Dan said as he hung up the phone.

The next day after driving Edith to the nursing home Dan went to the newest lawyer in town, Dave Wood. Dave greeted him at the door and immediately ushered Dan into his humble office. The diploma on the wall reflected graduation from the University of Montana Law School just one year before. Dan explained his desire to adopt Jeffey and the circumstances in which the father had surrendered his parental rights.

"This should be a fairly simple procedure," Dave explained thoughtfully. "I'll simply petition the court for you to adopt Jeffey. You'll probably have a hearing before Judge Milton Eubanks. If everything goes well, the court will grant the petition right away." Dave was unable to disguise his eagerness. "I'll get right on it and will let you know in a few days when the hearing will be."

"Thanks so much for your help," Dan said as he rose to

leave. "I'd like to make Jeffey my son the same time I make his mother my wife."

"I'll have to check the court calendar, but with your wedding date so close I can't guarantee anything."

The two men shook hands and Dan left the small office at the edge of town. He nearly floated down the steps. It would only be a matter of weeks before his dreams would come true.

ह

A week later after an extremely busy night at the crisis center, Dan collapsed on his bed at four o'clock in the morning. Scarcely a muscle twitched until the phone rang promptly at eight-thirty. Drowsily he reached for the receiver.

"Hello."

"Hello. Dan Blair, please."

"This is he. May I help you?"

"Dan, this is Dave Wood. I have some good news for you."

With those words Dan was immediately awake. "What is it?"

"I was able to get your day in court scheduled for June twenty-third at two o'clock."

"Thank you. Thank you so much," he stammered.

Dan hung up the phone and looked at the calendar. The big day was Saturday, June twenty-first. Beth's parents had agreed to come from Glasgow for the wedding and then stay with Jeffey while they took a ten-day honeymoon to Lake Coeur D'Alene, Idaho. *Surely, Beth won't mind postponing our departure for a couple of days so Jeffey could legally become my son,* he mused as he rolled over and fell back into a deep, peaceful sleep.

fifteen

Beth kicked off her shoes, sank into the sofa, and placed her feet on the ottoman. "Thank goodness Jeffey is asleep. It was a busy day at work and I'm beat."

"I wish there was something I could do to help," Dan replied as he put his arm around her shoulder.

"It's just something only Rebecca and I can trudge through," Beth sighed. "The end of the year inventory is bad enough, but with Rebecca retiring she's trying to teach me as much as possible and leave the library as well organized as possible for the new librarian."

"Have they hired anyone yet to replace her?"

"They've advertised locally and in all the statewide agencies and they've been amazed at the response. Since there have been so many budget cuts it seems like the libraries are the first place they cut and there's a lot of well-qualified school librarians out there," Beth explained. "Jobwise, I don't think this is a good time to be a school librarian. Rebecca did say they wanted to have someone hired before the last day of school."

"Even with school ending you're still going to be busy planning for the wedding, but at least that's something I can help you with," Dan replied.

"Just getting all the invitations addressed has become a real chore. I didn't realize we had so many friends and family until I began making a list," Beth smiled. "I hope everyone can come. I have a couple aunts that I haven't seen since I left Glasgow."

"Teresa Lennon has offered to take care of all the details for the reception, plus plan the decorations and flowers of the church. Why don't you take her up on the offer?" Dan suggested. "You have enough to do just getting yourself and Jeffey ready for the wedding."

"I hate to impose on her. Teresa has been so good to me."

"Teresa loves to plan social events," Dan coaxed. "It's her form of recreation. She'll be disappointed if she can't help."

"I suppose you're right," Beth responded. "I'll give her a call after work tomorrow and see if there's some time we can get together and plan the details. It sure would take a load off my mind if I didn't have the reception to worry about."

"After this is all over you're going to be ready for ten days of relaxation at Lake Coeur D'Alene. I already have our reservations made at the Pink Flamingo. We can sleep until noon, then rent a boat and cruise around the lake and admire the wildlife and the beautiful sunsets."

"That sounds heavenly, but it's going to be the first time I've been away from Jeffey since his kidnapping. I don't know how he's going to take it."

"Your mom and dad will be here and he'll be just fine," Dan reassured her. "You're the one who'll suffer separation anxiety."

"I suppose you're right," Beth laughed. "I know he is really looking forward to having a daddy."

"I wish we could go before the judge the day before the wedding instead of postponing the honeymoon for a couple of days, but it'll be well worth it. When we leave for

Coeur D'Alene he'll officially be my son. I've already checked into picking him up on my health insurance. There's no problem at all adding him.

"When we get back I'll just move my clothes over here and I'll put my extra things in a storage shed for a couple months until we move into Rebecca's house. My studio apartment isn't even big enough for one person, much less a family."

"I still can't get over the thought of living in a home as nice as Rebecca's and not having to pay a cent for the privilege."

"Don't forget you'll have to walk her dog and water her plants," Dan chided. "Nothing in life is ever free."

The pair continued their marriage discussion for another hour when Beth began to yawn and her eyes drooped. "Honey, I'd better let you get some sleep," Dan said. "I'll call you later tomorrow evening after you've talked with Teresa and see how things are going."

They embraced tenderly and Beth walked him to the door. "See you tomorrow," she murmured. "I love you."

"I love you too," he responded as he slipped out the front door.

❧

Beth and Jeffey had scarcely gotten in the door the next afternoon when the phone rang.

"Hello," Beth greeted as she laid her purse on the table.

"Hello, Beth, this is Teresa. How are you doing?"

"Keeping busy," she replied. "I was just getting ready to call you. How are you doing?"

"I'm doing well," Teresa replied. "I wanted to follow up on my offer. Is there anything I can do to help you with your wedding plans? I know it's hard work to follow through on all the multitude of details."

"Why don't you come over tonight or tomorrow evening and we could talk about the details? I'm feeling extremely overwhelmed right now."

"How about if I come over tonight at seven?" Teresa queried.

"Sounds good," Beth replied. "I'll be looking forward to it."

Beth had a pot of coffee and a plate of cookies waiting when Teresa arrived that evening. They discussed each aspect of the reception and decorations. Finally, Teresa became very serious, "Beth, what are you planning for a wedding dress?"

"I know the time is getting close, but I haven't decided," Beth admitted. "Even if I had the cash, I'd hate to put a lot of money in something I'll only wear once. Since it wouldn't be socially proper if I wore a pure white one I don't know what to do."

"I'll admit there isn't much of a selection here in Rocky Bluff," Teresa replied. "But I was talking with Rebecca last night and we thought that if you hadn't picked out a dress yet, we'd like to get one for you as our special wedding gift."

Beth was speechless and then began to stammer. "I. . . I couldn't let you do that for me. You've already done so much."

"It's something we'd really like to do," Teresa persisted. "Rebecca said that she doesn't know what she would have done without your help this past year. Don't deny us the chance of helping a good friend."

"How can I turn down that kind of offer?" Beth chuckled.

"You can't," Teresa replied firmly. "Now, what do you have planned for Saturday?"

"Just the usual. . .laundry, cleaning, and shopping."

"How about getting up early and the three of us going shopping in Great Falls? There's a real nice bridal shop there. I'm sure we could find a dress that would be just perfect for you. Time's a wasting."

"Sounds like fun," Beth agreed. "I'll see if Dan will be able to stay with Jeffey all day. If he's with Dan, I don't think he'll even miss me."

&

Edith Dutton had just finished eating lunch when the phone rang. "Hello."

"Hello, Edith. This is Larry Reynolds. How have you and Roy been doing?"

"I'm doing fine, but Roy seems to be failing more every day. I'll be seeing him this afternoon and hopefully he'll be better. Dan should be coming any time to take me to the nursing home."

"Good, maybe we'll see you there," Larry responded cheerfully.

"Are you at the nursing home now?"

"Not exactly. I'm next door at the hospital. Libby just had another baby girl at ten o'clock this morning."

Edith beamed. "Congratulations. How are they doing?"

"They're both great. She's the cutest little thing and already has a full head of hair. Vanessa was nearly bald until she was a year-and-a-half. She weighed in at seven pounds eight ounces."

"What did you name her?" Edith could scarcely contain her excitement.

"Charity Rae," Larry responded proudly. "We named

her that because she's a symbol of our new found love."

"That's beautiful. I'm so happy for you."

"I hope you can stop and see us while you're at the nursing home?" Larry queried.

"I wouldn't miss it for anything. What room is Libby in?"

"Room one-fifteen. They've already taken Charity to the nursery."

"Good, I'll see you within an hour," Edith promised and hung up the phone just as the door bell rang.

Edith hurried to the door. "Dan, do come in," she greeted. "I have some good news."

Dan's eyes widened with anticipation. It had been many weeks since he'd seen Edith this excited. "What's up?" he asked.

"Larry Reynolds just called. Libby had a baby girl this morning around ten. She weighed seven pounds eight ounces and they named her Charity Rae," Edith explained breathlessly. "Larry said they named her that because she was a symbol of their new love."

"Knowing what all they've been through as a family, that is the most fitting name possible for their baby," Dan observed. "I'd like to stop and see them when we go to the nursing home."

"Larry said they're in room one-fifteen. Would you mind waiting a minute until I find my Polaroid camera?"

Dan and Edith reminisced about the changes in Larry's and Libby's life on the way to the hospital. A new baby was the climax of years of struggling to find their way in life. As they entered the hospital room Larry was sitting in a chair beside the bed holding Libby's hand. Both their faces were radiant.

As soon as Larry was aware of someone else in the room he rose to greet them. "Edith, Dan, I'm so glad you could come."

"I wouldn't miss this for anything," Edith assured him and then turned her attention to Libby. "How are you doing?"

"I'm doing great," she beamed. "Have you been down the hall yet to see Charity?"

"Not yet. I wanted to see how you were doing first."

"I'll go with you," Libby responded as she started to get up from the hospital bed.

Larry took her arm firmly. "Wait just a minute and I'll get a wheelchair for you," he insisted. "You've worked hard enough for one day."

The new father proudly wheeled his wife down the hall of the Rocky Bluff Community Hospital with Edith and Dan close behind. They stopped in front of the nursery windows. Three babies were sleeping peacefully in their bassinets in front of the window.

"Charity is the one on the left," Larry stated. "Isn't she beautiful?"

"She sure is," Dan agreed as his eyes became distant. *Maybe in a year or two Beth and I will be standing in this same spot looking at our baby,* he mused.

"I can't tell which one of you she looks like the most," Edith commented as she studied the infant.

"I hope neither one of us," Larry chuckled. "We want her to be an even mix blend of both our good points and none of the bad."

Libby smiled up at Dan. "I'm glad Charity came this week. I didn't want to miss your wedding. Now we'll be able to take her and show her off."

"It wouldn't be complete without you and Larry," Dan chuckled. "However, I don't want your two adorable little girls upstaging my beautiful bride."

"Nothing could upstage Beth," Libby stated. "She's become simply radiant since she fell in love. You make a beautiful couple."

"They sure do," Edith agreed as she patted Dan's arm. "It's been a real pleasure to share these special moments with all of you." Edith paused and glanced back at the baby sleeping peacefully in the nursery. "If Roy's having a good day I'm sure he'd like to see Charity. Why don't I go down and see how he's doing?"

"We'd like to come with you. Larry's doing such a good job driving this chair," Libby chuckled. "I'm not used to having this kind of treatment."

When the foursome entered Roy's room he was sitting in his recliner watching TV. His eyes sparkled as soon as he saw that he had company and he immediately hit the mute button on the remote.

Edith leaned over and kissed him. "Hi Roy. How are you doing today?"

"G . . . g . . . g . . . ood."

"Libby and Larry just had a new baby," Edith explained with a smile.

Larry wheeled Libby's chair close enough so she could take Roy's hand. "She's a beautiful little girl whom we named Charity. Would you like to go see her?"

Roy smiled and nodded his head affirmatively.

Edith slipped out of the room and headed for the nurses' station. Within moments she returned with two nurses' aides and a wheelchair.

"I understand you want to go for a little outing," the

taller one said to Roy. "If you'll help us, we'll lift you into your wheelchair. It looks like you'll have a lot of help getting down to the nursery."

The nurses' aides gently lifted Roy and sat him in his wheelchair and adjusted the footrests.

"Enjoy yourself," they called as they disappeared down the hall to care for other residences.

"Roy receives such loving care here," Edith said. "I hate being separated from him, but I could never give him this kind of care at home. He still has a lot of friends stop to see him and every afternoon the activities director brings in different entertainment so he never gets bored."

The small band walked slowly down the hallway to the nursery. Larry pushed Libby's wheelchair while Dan pushed Roy's. Roy's eyes danced and a grin spread across his face as he looked through the window of the nursery.

"Save that look," Edith said as she took out her Polaroid camera.

With one click the photo session was on. Every possible grouping was made as the camera was passed from person to person. They waited for each picture to develop before deciding what grouping to take next. Finally a nurse came out of the nursery.

"Libby, would you like to have the baby in pictures as well?"

"We'd love to," Libby smiled. "I'd especially like to have one with Roy holding Charity. It would be one she could cherish for life."

The baby was brought out and gently laid in Roy's arms. Even his lack of speech could not prevent him from communicating the pleasure he felt at that moment. The camera clicked freely and only stopped long enough to add new film. Pictures were then taken of Roy and Edith with the baby. When it developed Larry replied, "This one I want to have framed. Without the loving guidance of both of you, I don't think there ever would be a Charity to bless our lives."

After the picture taking session Roy's eyes began to droop and his shoulders slumped. "Are you getting tired?" Edith asked.

Roy nodded. The small party of baby admirers bade each other good-bye. Larry wheeled Libby back to her room while Dan wheeled Roy down the long corridor to the nursing home with Edith at their side. Within minutes the same nurses' aides had Roy comfortably in his bed. Dan and Edith slipped quietly out of the room, down the long hall and out the front door. In spite of Roy's failing body, his spirit was still strong.

🕭

Promptly at two o'clock on the twenty-first of June the organist at Rocky Bluff Community Church began to play. Pastor Rhodes, Dan Blair, and two groomsmen entered from the side door and took their places in front of the congregation. One at a time two bridesmaids dressed in lavender strolled slowly down the aisle. Then Vanessa Reynolds came slowly down the aisle dropping petals as she came. She blew a kiss to her new sister as she passed her parents who were sitting on the aisle near the front of the church. Beside her was Jeffey Slater, dressed in a miniature tuxedo, carrying a pillow with a ring pinned to it. Jeffey beamed as soon as he saw Dan standing in the front. "How am I doing?" he whispered.

Everyone in the front snickered as they heard Dan whisper, "You're doing great, son."

The organ tempo increased as Mrs. Slater stood with the entire congregation following her lead. In the doorway stood Beth dressed in a beautiful off-white gown on the arm of her father. Her face grew radiant as she saw her fiance and her son waiting for her at the end of the aisle.

Beth scanned the room, the church was full. Nearly everyone she had invited was there. Her favorite aunts were sitting in the pew beside her mother. Edith Dutton was also included in the honored pew. Teresa had done a great job and the flowers, candles, and bows on the pews were perfect. Beth's eyes filled with tears. *God has been so good to me,* she mused. *Five years ago I was a scared unwed teenage mother with nowhere to go and no friends to turn to and now look at this.*

The next few minutes were a blur to Beth as her father escorted her up the aisle, the vocalist sang, and the pastor gave appropriate marital instructions. Her dream world was interrupted as she was staring into Dan's loving eyes and heard him say, "I, Dan, take thee, Beth, to be my wedded wife and Jeffey to be my precious son, to have and to hold from this day forward, for better for worse, for richer for poorer, in sickness and in health, to love and to cherish, till death us do part, according to God's holy ordinance; and thereto I pledge thee my faith."

Dan kissed his bride and picked up Jeffey and gave him a hug. "I love you, son," he whispered.

There was scarcely a dry eye in the church as Dan took Jeffey's hand in his and Beth took Dan's arm and they marched victoriously down the aisle into a new life as one family.

As the couple reached the door Pastor Rhodes lifted his arms in benediction. "What God has joined together, let no man put asunder."

A Letter To Our Readers

Dear Reader:

In order that we might better contribute to your reading enjoyment, we would appreciate your taking a few minutes to respond to the following questions. When completed, please return to the following:

Rebecca Germany, Editor
Heartsong Presents
P.O. Box 719
Uhrichsville, Ohio 44683

1. Did you enjoy reading *Inspired Love*?
   ❏ Very much. I would like to see more books
      by this author!
   ❏ Moderately
      I would have enjoyed it more if _____

   _____

2. Are you a member of *Heartsong Presents*? Yes   No
   If no, where did you purchase this book? _____

   _____

3. What influenced your decision to purchase this
   book? (Check those that apply.)

   ❏ Cover   ❏ Back cover copy

   ❏ Title   ❏ Friends

   ❏ Publicity   ❏ Other _____

4. On a scale from 1 (poor) to 10 (superior), please rate the following elements.

___Heroine   ___Plot

___Hero   ___Inspirational theme

___Setting   ___Secondary characters

5. What settings would you like to see covered in *Heartsong Presents* books?

_____

_____

6. What are some inspirational themes you would like to see treated in future books?_____

_____

_____

7. Would you be interested in reading other *Heartsong Presents* titles?   ❏ Yes   ❏ No

8. Please check your age range:
❏ Under 18   ❏ 18-24   ❏ 25-34
❏ 35-45   ❏ 46-55   ❏ Over 55

9. How many hours per week do you read? _____

Name _____

Occupation _____

Address _____

City _____ State _____ Zip _____

Susannah Hayden

❀❀❀❀❀❀❀❀❀❀❀❀❀❀❀❀❀❀❀❀❀❀❀❀❀❀❀❀

___*A Matter of Choice*—Stacie's new job promotion could mean the end of her future with Brad. . .or the start of a new and perhaps better life with Dillon. What life is Stacie to have? HP14

___*Between Love and Loyalty*—Megan Browning and her friends are working frantically to keep the old Homestead Youth Camp running. Then Megan discovers that the young architect who has captured her heart is planning on developing Homestead into condominiums. HP69

_*The Road Before Me*—Overwhelmed by self-doubt, Julie Covington searches for an answer. At her grandmother's childhood home in Maine she finds comfort and solace in the writings of a young girl, a girl who walked the same road as the one before Julie. HP77

___*Between the Memory and the Moment*—Jenna seems happy living and working at the camp owned by Dillon Graves. After all, she's hopelessly in love with the much-older Dillon, and he genuinely appreciates her work. Still, Jenna feels compelled to move on. But to what? HP113

___*Farther Along the Road*—Julie Covington wants to be accepted as a serious artist, and she wants to possess a love as vital as the one her grandmother had for her first love. When Larry Paxton displays interest in her paintings, Julie begins to feel hopeful that both needs can be fulfilled. HP117

..... Presents ....

__HP 65 ANGEL FACE, *Frances Carfi Matranga*
__HP 66 AUTUMN LOVE, *Ann Bell*
__HP 69 BETWEEN LOVE AND LOYALTY, *Susannah Hayden*
__HP 70 A NEW SONG, *Kathleen Yapp*
__HP 73 MIDSUMMER'S DREAM, *Rena Eastman*
__HP 74 SANTANONI SUNRISE, *Hope Irvin Marston and Claire M. Coughlin*
__HP 77 THE ROAD BEFORE ME, *Susannah Hayden*
__HP 78 A SIGN OF LOVE, *Veda Boyd Jones*
__HP 81 BETTER THAN FRIENDS, *Sally Laity*
__HP 82 SOUTHERN GENTLEMEN, *Yvonne Lehman*
__HP 85 LAMP IN DARKNESS, *Connie Loraine*
__HP 86 POCKETFUL OF LOVE, *Loree Lough*
__HP 89 CONTAGIOUS LOVE, *Ann Bell*
__HP 90 CATER TO A WHIM, *Norma Jean Lutz*
__HP 93 IDITAROD DREAM, *Janelle Jamison*
__HP 94 TO BE STRONG, *Carolyn R. Scheidies*
__HP 97 A MATCH MADE IN HEAVEN, *Kathleen Yapp*
__HP 98 BEAUTY FOR ASHES, *Becky Melby and Cathy Wienke*
__HP101 DAMAGED DREAMS, *Mary Hawkins*
__HP102 IF GIVEN A CHOICE, *Tracie J. Peterson*
__HP105 CIRCLE OF LOVE, *Alma Blair*
__HP106 RAGDOLL, *Kelly R. Stevens*
__HP109 INSPIRED LOVE, *Ann Bell*
__HP110 CALLIE'S MOUNTAIN, *Veda Boyd Jones*

Great Inspirational Romance at a Great Price!

Heartsong Presents books are inspirational romances in contemporary and historical settings, designed to give you an enjoyable, spirit-lifting reading experience. You can choose from 112 wonderfully written titles from some of today's best authors like Colleen L. Reece, Brenda Bancroft, Janelle Jamison, and many others.

When ordering quantities less than twelve, above titles are $2.95 each.

SEND TO: Heartsong Presents Reader's Service
P.O. Box 719, Uhrichsville, Ohio 44683

Please send me the items checked above. I am enclosing $ _____
(please add $1.00 to cover postage per order. OH add 6.25% tax. NJ add 6%.). Send check or money order, no cash or C.O.D.s, please.
   To place a credit card order, call 1-800-847-8270.

NAME _____

ADDRESS _____

CITY/STATE_____ ZIP _____

HPS FEBRUARY